BEHIND
Closed Doors

Kiki Swinson

Publisher's address:

K.S. Publications
P.O. Box 68878
Virginia Beach, VA 23471

Website: www.KikiMedia.net
Email: KS.publications@yahoo.com
ISBN-13: 978-1733919029
ISBN-10: 1-7339190-2-3

First Edition: November 2019

10 9 8 7 6 5 4 3 2 1

Editors: Letitia Carrington
Book-cover Design: Mariondesigns.com
Interior Design: Mariondesigns.com

Printed in the U.S.A

BEHIND
Closed Doors

Kiki Swinson

KS Publications
www.KikiMedia.net

To My Dear Husband, Mr. Julian "Juice" Seay…. What could I say to let the whole world know that you are my everything. It seems like yesterday when we met at the mall outside the Bass Pro Shop on Easter Sunday in 2015. You told me that you instantly fell in love with me. I didn't believe you then but I believe you now. I mean, look at me…. I am pretty, smart, funny and in love with you! With that said, just now that I will never stop loving you! Congrats on your new book My Time to Shine! Now let's get that book in everyone's hands.

Love Always,

Wifey

Don't Miss Out On These Other Titles:

BEHIND
Closed Doors

Kiki Swinson

Chapter One
My Screwed Up Life

The sun sparkled over the Epstein family's summer home in the Hamptons. The sunlit lawn is why they'd chosen the property. The home was a huge mansion in an exclusive gated community, sat on top of a hill with gorgeous views from every room. The natural sunlight hit the well-manicured lawn like a movie spotlight. Evelyn Epstein stood with her arms folded across her chest, staring out at the massive landscape. She inhaled the fresh scent of the newly cut grass and let out a long-exasperated breath. She had so much on her mind. Evelyn and her family had been coming to the Hamptons from New York City each summer for eighteen years now, and with every passing year, the façade they put on of the perfect little family seemed to crack a little more. She shuddered just thinking about how much things had crumbled. No more picture-perfect life for Evelyn a thought that made her want to cry.

This summer was the worst it had ever been. Evelyn had walked hand and hand with her husband Levi into the high-class house parties of the Hampton's elite, although her marriage was all but over. It had been at her urging that they acted as if things were still wonderful at home. Evelyn had also smiled, chuckled and told several people that her daughter was away in Europe studying anthropology, although her only child was tucked away from the probing eyes in drug rehab four hours away from the Hamptons. The best lie of all, however; was how Evelyn had played the role of a happy-go-lucky, faithful wife, although she had been plotting for months on how to get even with her husband by finding her own love affair. Evelyn had to admit, this time she felt more powerful than she ever had during her entire marriage. Yes, it was a crazy time at the Epstein home. Evelyn didn't know how much more of a horse and pony show she could put on for all of her superficial, "happily married" friends. She was dying slowly inside. The fake smiles and all of the lies were wearing on her. She had literally watched her perfect life fade into obscurity. She was in a loveless marriage; her only child was a drug addict; and, now she had found out how her husband had been keeping them afloat financially all of these years since his family had shut him out of his late father's wealth. Things were spiraling downward fast. Evelyn had always thought of herself as being in full control of it all. Not now. The reality of just how little control she had was never more evident than now.

Evelyn closed her eyes when she heard Levi approaching from behind. She smelled his signature, Ralph Lauren Safari cologne before he even made it to where she stood. She flinched as Levi placed one hand on her shoulder and pecked her on her cheek. More like a brother would perfunctorily kiss his sister. "How are you?" he asked dryly. Evelyn cracked a halfhearted smile, her back going rigid and her shoulders stiffening under his touch. It was all she could do to keep her composure, to keep from punching, slapping, and spitting on him. She couldn't find one ounce of love left for her husband. Their once undying love had withered into contempt, resentments, and regrets. She was sure Levi could tell from her body language that she wasn't up for any small talk from him.

"You're up early," Levi commented, flashing a perfectly veneered fake smile. Levi wasn't going to let Evelyn kill his refreshed spirit with her normal sour mood. He never looked Evelyn in the eyes anymore. She knew it was because of his guilt for his latest conquest. "I guess you have your day planned already..." he continued the small talk with no response from Evelyn. He set something down next to him and by Evelyn's side. That got her attention right away. She looked down and peered at Levi's suitcase. She rolled her eyes and bit into her bottom lip. She could feel the heat rising from her chest, and her hands involuntarily curled into fists. Levi noticed his wife's body language. He wore an expression that said not again. The manufactured drama was getting old fast.

"I won't be gone long. I promise. I'll be back in time for Diane's annual all-white affair. I know how much that means to you," Levi explained, dryly garnering no response in his wife's body language. He knew that keeping up appearances for her friends was more important to Evelyn than anything he could ever do to make her happy again. Evelyn turned towards Levi abruptly, causing him to take a step back. She moved in like a lion towards its prey, her eyes in evil slits.

"Did you forget your daughter is graduating from the rehabilitation center today?" Evelyn asked, her voice low, almost a growl. She eyed him evilly, her nostrils moving in and out. She had one shaky finger jutted accusingly towards Levi, and her other hand balled so tightly her nails dug moon-shaped craters into her palms. She was tired of playing second fiddle in Levi's life. But, if he was going to treat her like she didn't exist…fine, but now their only child.

"I didn't forget. I told you I have a very important business meeting," he replied, annoyed. "I left her a gift on the table inside. There's a note there and a little something to make up for my absence," Levi finished flatly without looking his wife in the eyes. He immediately signaled for his driver to grab his bags. In his assessment, there was nothing else to talk about. Levi knew how their confrontations would end up. He had long since grown tired of Evelyn's constant guilt trips and self-pity parties. She had definitely become a shell of her former vibrant, outgoing, attention-commanding self. She was far from the woman he'd married.

"So that's it? You throw money at her again? A goddamn note Levi?! Is that all you can offer her?! You think a note can make up for your absence?!" Are we back to our same antics again? Your family comes second to the new whore!" Evelyn barked at her husband's back. "It was your money that got her where she is in the first place!" Levi gave her a look that sent a chill down her spine before he continued on.

"Levi! I am talking to you!" Evelyn called out again. He ignored her and rushed down the front steps. Before she could say another word, Levi climbed into the back of his Mercedes May Bach and slammed the door. Evelyn rocked on her heels as she watched the car ease down the long pathway towards the road. That was it. Just like that, Levi was gone again.

Evelyn had been through the same thing so many times she had come to expect it. She had recognized all of the signs that Levi was having yet another affair. It had been a month

4

since she'd gotten the photographs from the private investigator that had confirmed her suspicions. This time Levi had crossed the line; he'd gotten disrespectful and disgusting with his philandering. When Evelyn had reviewed the photos of Levi and his new mistress, she'd thrown up the entire contents of her stomach. The same gut sickening feeling had come over her again, but this time was different…more personal.

Evelyn could feel her heart throbbing against her chest bone now just thinking about it. She guessed this was what a broken heart felt like. It wasn't a new feeling, and she didn't know why it always felt like a fresh wound. Evelyn silently chastised herself for being so emotional all of the time. It had been twenty-two years since she'd met and married who she thought was the man of her dreams and he'd been unfaithful at least ten or more of those years. She closed her eyes to stifle the angry tears threatening to fall. Instead, she headed into the house to make a phone call. "Two can play the game this time around Levi Epstein," she mumbled as she stormed through the house. There would be no more victim roll for Evelyn. No. She planned to be victorious this time around.

Evelyn had just stepped off the runway at New York's Fashion week when she'd first met Levi in 1989. Evelyn's perfect ivory skin went flush with red when Levi approached her at the after-show reception. Everyone who was anyone in New York City knew who Levi Epstein was—the gorgeous and very wealthy son of Ari Epstein, New York's most wealthy real estate tycoon. It was a well-known fact that Levi Epstein could have any woman in the world he wanted. Not only was he strikingly attractive, he was rich and single, and the opportunities that came his way were abundant. He was thirty-five and number one on the most eligible bachelor list; a fact that was not lost on Evelyn when Levi approached her flashing his perfect smile and displaying the charm of a storybook prince. He immediately grabbed her hand and planted his perfect lips on the top of it. It was something like electricity that had coursed through Evelyn's body, but she had done a fabulous job of keeping her composure.

Standing together, they looked like the perfect Hollywood couple. Evelyn's statuesque six-foot frame was adorned with a beautiful, teal, Donna Karan dress that dipped low in the back exposing her firm, muscular frame. The dress had fit her svelte body like it had been sewn on. Perfectly coifed, dark brown, ringlets of hair danced around her face and picked up the chestnut in her eyes.

"You were stunning in the show," Levi had said to her. His smile was a lady-killer. Evelyn had felt a whoosh of breath leave her lungs in response to his smooth baritone. Although she looked like a grown woman, Evelyn was only nineteen years old and hadn't had much time to date. Levi's beautiful grey eyes and his neatly trimmed jet-black hair had overwhelmed her. He reminded Evelyn of a younger Brad Pitt. Looking at him made her pulse quicken, so she lowered her eyes, stared down into her drink, and smiled girlishly.

"You probably say that to all of the models," Evelyn murmured, still averting direct eye contact. Levi had placed his finger under her chin and urged her to look at him. Evelyn reluctantly locked eyes with him, and when he smiled, she swore she could feel her heart-melting. Standing in his presence, Evelyn felt like they were the only two people in the large, crowded ballroom. They'd spent the entire reception laughing and talking about everything from runway fashions to politics. Levi had asked Evelyn if he could call her sometime and maybe take her out. She'd told him that she was leaving for Milan the next day and would be gone for two months. Levi had told her that was all the more reason he wanted to get to know her—she was a woman with her own life. He'd asked if she would leave her contact information so that he could call her sometime. She scribbled her information down on a silver trimmed napkin. Levi pushed it into his lapel pocket. "Right next to my heart," he'd said, tapping the place where he had put her number. That made Evelyn blush all over again. She was smitten.

After her third day in Milan, Evelyn returned to her hotel one night to find the entire room filled with beautiful long stem pink, red, and white roses. She was flabbergasted when she'd read the card, "You are as pretty as a newly blossomed rose. I came to Milan just to see you. Please call. Levi Epstein."

Evelyn had flopped down on her bed, weak with joy. The other two lanky beauties she had been rooming with snickered and made love faces and googly eyes at her. "Call him! Call him," They had twirled around her, urging her to call Levi right away, but Evelyn opted to wait until the next day. She didn't want him to think she was that easy to win over. When she'd finally called, Levi officially asked her out on a date. They went on their first date, and it had been magical—a gondola ride, dinner at a quaint Italian eatery, and a romantic walk through the city at night. Evelyn was overwhelmed with feelings she'd never experienced in her life. It had to be love.

Levi had wanted to know all about her life. He'd been the first man to ever care about the little things that mattered to her, like her childhood and how she'd become a high fashion model at such a young age. They spent another night talking into the wee hours of the morning. It was like they had been made for each other from the start. Evelyn had never experienced anything like what she had that night. No one had ever shown her the kind of interest that Levi had shown her. Levi felt the same as well. He had always had women swooning over him, but none had ever held his interest as long as Evelyn had. It was like a fateful love that was meant to be from the start.

Levi stayed in Milan for a week wining and dining Evelyn after her fashion photoshoots and shows. He wanted to make sure that she knew that he wanted her; that he was interested in her; and that, he intended on making this a regular occurrence. He'd showered her with beautiful premier designer gifts. Levi had spared no expense. He felt like it was the least he could do for this beauty he had found. Before he left Milan, Levi asked Evelyn to call him when she returned to New York. She had initially acted as if she had had to "think about it," but Evelyn knew the real truth about how she was feeling inside. She could hardly sit still for her entire flight from Milan to New York City. Evelyn had called as soon as her plane landed at JFK Airport. Her hands had trembled as she had dialed his number from a cold payphone right inside of the airport. Evelyn was relieved when he'd answered. She literally melted inside once she was able to speak to the man; she knew she was falling in love with. Levi was all she could think of for the time she remained in Milan without him. She had crazy feelings of longing. So much so that the other girls had teased her incessantly until their job in Milan was done.

Evelyn and Levi met the day after her return to New York, and they had officially begun dating. Levi had given her a single flower he'd picked from Central Park and said, "would you be mine?" They had shared a hearty laugh at Levi's antics, but Evelyn had surely accepted the little wilting flower and his invitation to date him.

Levi made Evelyn feel like she was the only woman in the world every single day. There was never a dull moment with him. Not only did he shower her with gifts, but he'd taken her to all of New York's most exclusive invite-only social events and acted as if he was so proud to have her on his arm. Levi was such a gentleman. He was extremely, loving, and he paid attention to every detail of their relationship. People always commented "on what a beautiful couple they made. After a year of dating, Levi finally proposed. When he'd presented Evelyn with his great grandmother's sapphire and diamond engagement ring, Evelyn almost wet herself. She jumped into his arms screaming, "yes! yes! yes!" Levi's parents weren't happy with his choice. They would have preferred a good, clean, Jewish girl for their youngest son. Evelyn had grown up Catholic. She was certainly no virgin if she was a model; Levi's mother had complained. Evelyn also didn't have parents, which alarmed the Epsteins. "What is a girl without a mother?! No mother, no religion, what else Levi!" Levi's mother had screamed in her usual theatrical performance manner. Levi had heard his mother's "dream girl" for him so many times that he went out and found the complete opposite.

Evelyn so head over heels in love quickly agreed to go through the process of converting to Judaism. Levi's parents; defeated by Evelyn and Levi's love; finally settled. Evelyn and Levi were married in a traditional Jewish ceremony. The wedding took place on a white sand beach adjacent to Ari

Epstein's $40 million-dollar estate in the Caribbean island of Turks and Caicos. Four hundred guests attended the lavish wedding; of which, only twenty-five were Evelyn's friends—people she'd befriended while modeling. The remainder of the guests she'd never even met. At the time, Evelyn didn't dare complain. She felt like she was living a dream; far from what she could have ever envisioned for herself. As an orphan who'd grown up poor, Evelyn never dreamed she'd become a world-renowned model, but more importantly, that she'd be married to one of the most coveted men in the United States. On all accounts, Evelyn thought she'd walked into heaven. It didn't take long for her to realize she'd been sadly mistaken. Life with Levi had changed so drastically, sometimes Evelyn couldn't believe he was the same man she'd met back then.

"Mrs. Epstein your car is out front," Carolynn announced snapping Evelyn out of her reverie. Evelyn hadn't even realized she'd been staring into space. She quickly dabbed at her eyes and turned towards Carolynn. Carolynn smiled at her, realizing she had interrupted Evelyn's thoughts.

"I want everything to be perfect for Arianna when she gets here. Please make sure the caterers are on time and the tent…the decorations have to be perfect. Her favorite color is blue. The cake is supposed to be delivered in two hours. The guests should arrive…I just…" Evelyn rambled; an edge of nerves apparent in her words. Carolynn put her hand up and let a warm smile spread across her face. She knew her boss was nervous.

"Mrs. E, I will have everything in order. I know how important this day is to you and to Ari," Carolynn comforted, her warm smile easing the tension in the air. Evelyn exhaled and thanked Carolynn. She trusted Carolynn who'd worked for the family since Arianna was born. Only, Evelyn, Levi, and Carolynn knew the truth about the purpose of the big party. Carolynn knew all of the family's secrets. She had become a part of their family; thus, she knew every detail of their lives. She followed Evelyn around the huge master suite making sure Evelyn didn't forget anything. Carolynn gave the room a once over. Everything seemed to be all right.

Evelyn grabbed her Hermes Birkin and looked at herself one last time in the long Victorian-style mirror that took up almost an entire wall in the master suite. She was still a knockout, even at forty-one years old. Admittedly, she had a little help from one of the top plastic surgeons in New York, a nip here and a tuck there, but her natural beauty still came through. Her face showed only a few crow's feet at the corners of her eyes, nothing a little Restylane couldn't cure she thought. She'd just gotten rid of her laugh lines a week prior, and she'd gotten her lips filled in while she was at it. Evelyn had opted to use collagen fillers instead of Botox-like most of her friends. Carolynn smiled as she watched her boss go over her outfit again and again. It was a habit Evelyn hadn't broken in all these years. Carolynn knew Evelyn's next move before she even did it. Just as anticipated, Evelyn ran her hands over the flat part of her stomach and turned sideways to make sure her Spanx were doing their job. It was flat as a board. Perfect.

She wore a pair of white, wide-legged crepe Versace sailor pants that complimented her long, still model-like slim legs. Carolyn assisted Evelyn as she shrugged into a short, navy Diane Von Furstenberg blazer to complete her look. Evelyn adjusted her newly lifted D cup breasts and examined her neck and jaw lines to make sure her tanning bed hadn't left any streaks. She smiled at herself and then back at Carolynn.

"Not so bad for the mother of an eighteen-year-old, huh Carolynn?" Evelyn posed the question she really didn't want the answer to.

"Beautiful," Carolynn praised on queue. They'd had this same routine for the longest.

Evelyn chuckled. She knew she was the quintessential kept woman. Through it all, she had managed to keep herself in tiptop shape, and with the assistance of her plastic surgeon, she still got mistaken for a woman in her thirties. As she headed out of the house towards her waiting ride, her cell phone buzzed in her bag. Evelyn fished around and retrieved it. Instinctively a smile spread across her face. "Hello lover," she cooed into the mobile device as she slid into the back of the Bentley that awaited her. Evelyn closed her eyes; maybe the day wouldn't be as bad as she'd thought it would be. Especially if she could slip away after she did her motherly duty.

Chapter Two
Family First

*P*eople rushed around her, but that didn't distract Evelyn at all. She kept her head up high as she sat on one of the hard-wooden seats inside the auditorium of the Passages Rehabilitation Center. Her palms were sweaty, and she couldn't keep her legs from rocking back and forth. Evelyn was clearly out of her element, but she knew she had to be there regardless. She kept telling herself, "it is my duty."

Evelyn looked around at some of the parents there, just like her, most seemed to be well off. Evelyn tried not to stare too long, but she couldn't help it. She felt a pang of jealousy looking at some of the couples holding hands and being supportive of each other. Seemingly happy families made her stomach churn. She wished that were her life again. Damn you, Levi.

Evelyn shook her head to clear it and tried to focus on why she was there—for her child. Her only child. And it had cost them $100,000 to get Arianna the treatment she needed. It was an expense neither Evelyn nor Levi could argue wasn't necessary. Private drug rehabilitation was expensive, but in Evelyn's assessment, there was no amount of money that could keep her from trying to save her daughter or save face with her friends was more like it. There was no way Evelyn could stand for any of her socialite friends to find out Arianna was addicted to drugs and had been living like a virtual vagabond. The thought of anyone finding out made a cold chill shoot down Evelyn's spine. She hunched her shoulders in an attempt to relax, but the thoughts still hovered.

Evelyn remembered clearly how devastated she was when she found out their princess was addicted to methamphetamine. It was Carolynn who'd nervously told Evelyn about Arianna's addiction. Evelyn also thought back to how Levi had screamed at her and told her it was all her fault that his daughter was an embarrassment to the Epstein name. He had told Evelyn it was Evelyn's "trashy" DNA and family lineage that had caused their daughter to be such a disappointment. It hadn't been the first time Levi had used Evelyn's upbringing against her during an argument.

"Mother," Evelyn heard the familiar voice from behind her. She popped up out of her seat and cleared away the thoughts that had been crowding her mind. Evelyn took in an eyeful of her only child. She tilted her head and clasped her hand over her mouth. Tears welled up in her eyes immediately when she went to grab for her daughter.

"Oh, sweetheart…you look amazing. This time away has done wonders. I am so proud of you," Evelyn cried, grabbing her daughter in a tight embrace. Evelyn felt a warm feeling of relief wash over her. Arianna finally presented like something Evelyn could be proud of. Evelyn squeezed Arianna again. "Thank God," she whispered. Evelyn was really thanking God for bringing her daughter back from the brink of death. What would her friends have thought if Arianna had gave way to a drug addiction? Evelyn would've suffered the worst embarrassment of her life. Evelyn shook off those worse case scenarios and tried to relish in the moment.

It was a miracle that Arianna was even alive. The night Evelyn and Levi had signed Arianna into the rehabilitation center involuntarily, Arianna had looked like death warmed over. Her skin had been ghostly pale, and dark rings rimmed the bottoms of her eyes. Arianna's dark hair had been matted in clumps around her scalp, and her body was gaunt, almost skeletal. She smelled like she hadn't had a bath in weeks and her clothes, although expensive, were filthy. Arianna had been out on a binge for three weeks while Evelyn and Levi worried sick and had people out scouring the entire city for her. It had been the first time they'd come together for anything in years. Levi had even hugged Evelyn a few of the nights they'd both sat up worrying about their daughter. Arianna had kicked and screamed when she'd first arrived at the center. She cursed at her parents and told her mother she hated her. She'd screamed and begged Levi not to let Evelyn sign her into the center. Arianna blamed Evelyn for everything. Evelyn was an emotional wreck that night. She also blamed herself for it all, although she knew it wasn't entirely her fault. Levi had remained cool as a cucumber, as usual. "Daddy loves you. Daddy loves you," Levi had repeated to his daughter over and over again. He never once defended Evelyn and told his daughter she needed the help. It was something Evelyn filed in her mental Rolodex. The hurt she'd felt was almost tangible.

All of that was the past Evelyn told herself now. Just like all of the other hurts she'd suffered at the hands of her daughter and husband, Evelyn swallowed them like hard marbles. Seeing

15

Arianna now—cheeks rosy, body filled out in all of the right places, hair shiny and straight, made Evelyn warm inside. Arianna had taken the best of Evelyn and Levi's features. She stood almost six feet tall and was built like a runway model. She had long slender legs, a small waist, and small breasts. Arianna had exquisite, thick, jet-black hair and slate grey eyes. She had inherited Evelyn's high cheekbones and perfect nose, and with Levi's prominent chin, her face was striking. From the time she was a small child, Arianna had turned heads everywhere she went. She was more of a showstopper than both of her parents to say the least.

Evelyn finally relinquished her grasp on Arianna and gave her a good once over. Evelyn smiled wide; she thought her daughter looked perfect. Arianna was dressed conservatively in a maroon Donna Karan sheath dress that Carolynn had picked out; a pair of kitten-heeled Jimmy Choo's and a simple cardigan to top off her look. Arianna finally looked like an eighteen-year-old wealthy J.A.P (Jewish American Princess) should. Evelyn was satisfied, but she still couldn't say she was ever proud to say that Arianna was her daughter. It had always been a struggle being a mother to Arianna. Evelyn squeezed Arianna and grabbed for Arianna's hand, hoping to get a return show of affection. But Arianna impolitely let her arms hang limp at her side. Evelyn knew right away that her daughter was in rare form. It was the norm for Arianna to treat Evelyn like she had no regard for her at all.

"Where's dad?" Arianna asked petulantly. Evelyn released her daughter's hand quickly. She looked at Arianna seriously. She wanted to scream in Arianna's face and say I am here for you! Isn't that enough! He was never there for you like I have been! But Evelyn kept her thoughts to herself; kept smiling and kept doing what she did best—pretending.

"Oh, Ari darling, this is your day. Don't worry about the small things. You look so good...so healthy now," Evelyn replied sympathetically. She cracked a phony smile and hugged her daughter again, hoping they could move off the subject of Levi. "You are simply stunning Ari, I can't say that enough," Evelyn followed up, flashing her plastic smile again. Nothing seemed to faze Arianna.

"I guess you would say I look good now since you haven't seen me in six months. All you have to compare it to is the way I looked when you forced me into this hell hole," Arianna replied sharply, as she squirmed out of her mother's stifling embrace. Evelyn felt like someone had slapped her across the face. She inhaled. It was taking all she had to keep it together now.

Evelyn ignored the comment. She already felt awful enough about not visiting, but she'd figured that Arianna needed time away without the influence of her parents. Evelyn had been afraid that if she'd visited, Arianna would ask her questions about her father. Evelyn had always tried to shelter Arianna from the reality that her father was a philandering whore. Evelyn's sugar-coating Levi's indiscretions only made Arianna see Evelyn as the bad guy and Levi as the hero in their lives. The past six months had been no different. Levi cheated, and Evelyn covered up. She hid his ways from Arianna; their friends; his parents... everyone. It became like a fulltime job for Evelyn. Faking, like her life, was still picture perfect. This time was slightly different. Now as Arianna shot accusing eyes at her, Evelyn guiltily thought about her own preoccupation while her daughter was gone and wanted to veer away from the topic of why she didn't visit.

"So are you ready to go home? You must be excited to get back to life. There are so many good things waiting for you. Whatever you want, you can have," Evelyn asked, changing the subject while fidgeting with her newly purchased monstrous twelve-carat canary diamond ring. It was one of many things she'd purchased on spite after finding out the identity of Levi's most recent mistress.

"Yeah going home…I can hardly wait to get back to that life. I'll see you after the ceremony," Arianna droned gruffly, stomping away from her mother. Evelyn looked around to see if anyone had noticed the strained interaction between them. She smiled weakly at a couple that had been watching. Evelyn's cheeks flamed over when she noticed them. She wondered how much of the conversation they had overheard. "These children. We have to love them," Evelyn chortled, averting her eyes away from the gawking pair. She turned her face away and dabbed at the tears threatening to drop from her eyes. Even her baby girl hated her. Evelyn couldn't win for trying. Nothing was ever good enough for Arianna and Levi. Years later, she still couldn't please them.

The night Arianna was born Levi had missed the entire birth—from labor to the minute Arianna took her first breath. Evelyn had spent sixteen hours in labor at Lenox Hill Hospital, and Levi never showed up for a minute of it. Both of Levi's parents had come rushing into Evelyn's private birthing room in a huff when they'd gotten the news that their newest member was about to arrive. But neither of them could explain why their son hadn't been around when Evelyn tried to reach him. Levi's parents had long since stopped making excuses for Levi because they knew Evelyn wasn't buying it anymore. Evelyn felt that their presence at the birth was only because they secretly hoped she would provide them with a grandson to carry on the Epstein name. Evelyn had known for months she was carrying a baby girl, but she never told Levi or his parents. She knew how Jews really felt about having first-born girls. She also knew they only tolerated her as it was. Evelyn hadn't felt that alone in a room full of people since her days living in an orphanage. Nurses, Levi's parents, doctors, all circled around her, providing for her every need. But no one could soothe the ache of loneliness she felt for Levi.

After a horrendous labor, Evelyn had given birth to a perfect little girl through cesarean section. She'd made sure she got her tummy tucked at the same time. She wouldn't have wanted to disappoint Levi by not keeping herself up. Evelyn had already suspected that Levi was stepping out with other women behind her back.

The baby girl was a perfect, pink-faced, screaming bundle of joy. She had Levi's grey eyes and prominent chin, with Evelyn's long limbs and button nose. "Let's call her Ari… after her grandfather," Levi's mother had said after she laid eyes on her granddaughter. Ari Epstein, Levi's father agreed and who was Evelyn to argue with such a powerful patriarch. Whatever the Epsteins wanted, the Epsteins got. Evelyn had learned that the hard way. The naming of her first child would be no different. Evelyn, too physically and mentally exhausted to protest, compromised with the Epstein's and they all agreed to call the baby, Arianna Bethany Epstein. Or baby Ari for short. Evelyn thought it was a fair compromise given the fact that she had always wanted to name her first daughter Beth Ann, after a mother she had never known. She never told the Epsteins of her desires; instead, she came up with a name she thought she could live with.

When Levi finally showed up at the hospital to see his new baby, he smelled of a woman's perfume and looked like he'd been partying for days. He leaned in to give Evelyn an obligatory kiss, and she had turned her face away. It was all she could do to keep from making a scene in front of Levi's parents and to hide the hot tears that were threatening to spring from her eyes. Evelyn had tried to hold onto her anger and bitterness that first night Levi came to her bedside, but, after witnessing Levi hold his daughter with such care and sensitivity and watching him seemingly fall in love with his daughter, Evelyn had been overwhelmed with that old, gushy, head-over-heels feeling for Levi once again. It was like when they were in Milan, falling in love all over again. Evelyn had told herself that night in the hospital that for her child and the sake of her family, she would do anything it took to make them happy. It was a promise she would come to suffer to keep.

Things were great for a while after Arianna's birth. Evelyn felt like she'd finally gotten her husband back. In the beginning, Levi was a doting father and a caring husband. He showered Evelyn with gift after expensive gift. He'd told her the gifts were to thank her for giving him his greatest gift of all. He spent hours holding baby Ari, talking, and singing to her. So much so, Evelyn had shamefully grown a little jealous of how much attention Levi showered on the baby. But once again, Evelyn put her feelings aside and tried to make the best of the situation. Evelyn saw herself as just mother and wife.

There was no more individual Evelyn. The things she wanted, needed and liked came secondary in her life. Evelyn spent every waking minute pleasing her daughter and her husband. She'd lost herself in meeting the needs of Levi and Arianna. But it was with the help of the hired hands of course. At some point, Evelyn grew to resent her life. Each day, she would perfunctorily put on a happy face.

As Arianna grew older, Evelyn and Levi gave her anything she asked for…materially anyway. From birth, Arianna was a trust fund baby. She was worth more than some celebrities five times her age, and she hadn't even turned a year old. Papa Epstein, which is what Levi's father asked to be called, had made sure his granddaughter would never have to lift a finger in her life. Evelyn felt a sense of security knowing that unlike herself as a child, her daughter would never want for anything.

There were extravagant nurseries built for baby Ari in every home Levi owned, even in his two New York City penthouses. Arianna was royalty in the eyes of the entire Epstein family. She had been given dance lessons from the age of two. She had a private acting coach as soon as she turned five. Papa Ari purchased a thoroughbred riding horse for Arianna's tenth birthday and equestrian lessons to match. She'd had huge, extravagant birthday parties every year with a guest list of A-list celebrity children. For her Bat Mitzvah, they'd flown in dresses from Paris, Milan, and London. Once a year Evelyn and Levi would take Arianna on vacation to parts of the world she couldn't even pronounce. Private schools were the only kind ever considered for Arianna. She'd been provided an allowance of $1,000 per week from the time she was thirteen years old. Even after the huge Bat Mitzvah, Arianna's sweet sixteen was thrown on a yacht and cost more than some celebrity weddings. But, as she got older, Arianna realized that nothing her parents gave her could replace spending time with them every day or having at least one sit down dinner with them like she'd seen done in families on television. Carolynn was the person who showed up for school meetings, plays, and trips. Levi and Evelyn hardly knew anything concrete about their daughter's wants and needs. Evelyn was too busy keeping tabs on Levi to notice.

After a while, nothing Levi and Evelyn gave Arianna seemed like enough. They poured money into any activity she picked up—gymnastics, soccer, synchronized swimming, lacrosse, equestrian, golf, polo, and, tennis. Arianna would grow bored and quit. She had grown to be spoiled and angry. By the time she was seventeen, Arianna was deep into the New York party and drug scene. She fashioned herself as one of New York City's brat pack socialites. Late night party scenes became her daily life. She'd grown up and become best friends with former child stars, daughters of hotel magnates and children of rock stars. Unflattering paparazzi pictures of Arianna had shown up at least two dozen times in People and Us magazines. When confronted, Arianna would scream and throw tantrums. Evelyn had admittedly dropped the ball when it came to paying her daughter the attention she was craving. But she blamed Levi for it all, and he blamed her just the same.

Evelyn and Arianna's ride from the rehabilitation center was tensely silent. It was as if a joyous occasion had not just happened. Arianna was brooding the entire ride, and Evelyn was trying to please as usual. The pomp and circumstance of Arianna's rehab graduation faded quicker than an eclipse of the sun. Afterward, Evelyn had tried to make small talk, about the weather, Arianna's clothes, her new cell phone. When that didn't work, Evelyn tried to tell Arianna how proud she was of her accomplishments—getting clean and sober in six months. Evelyn had told Arianna that she imagined it hadn't been easy. Arianna ignored her mother, for the most part, dropping a vicious insult in response here and there. It wasn't lost on either of them how many times Evelyn's cell phone had buzzed and interrupted their tense exchange. Arianna had even raised an eyebrow to her mother and said, "Why don't you stop pretending to be interested in speaking to me and just answer your phone?" Evelyn's cheeks had flamed over at her daughter's comment. "No one is more important that you Ari," Evelyn had replied. It didn't make a difference. She was clearly not going to make Arianna happy.

Finally, too exasperated to continue practically begging her daughter to talk to her, Evelyn gave up. Arianna rudely put her iPod earphones in and turned the volume up so loud Evelyn could hear every curse word in the lyrics of the rock music she listened to. Arianna also took to texting incessantly on her cell phone, one of the luxuries she had missed while locked up in that place. Defeated, Evelyn resorted to watching the passing scenery outside of the Bentley's darkly tinted windows. Evelyn secretly wished she were someplace else. She could think of a million things she would've rather be doing than taking her daughter's verbal abuse. Evelyn's mind drifted to things she found pleasurable. Of course, she thought about Max, her new friend. The thoughts seemed to ease the pain of the long ride. Evelyn found herself growing a little flush with some of the thoughts Max conjured in her mind.

When the car pulled up to the gate leading up to the house, Arianna yanked her earphones out of her ears and bolted upright in her seat. "I'm not going to the summer house, I'm going to the city...the penthouse," she announced brusquely. Evelyn's eyebrows shot up, and her pulse sped up. Arianna had been practically living alone at their Upper East Side penthouse when she'd disappeared and ultimately gotten herself in trouble. Evelyn didn't think it was a good idea for her to go back into that environment so soon. Evelyn wanted Carolynn to keep an eye on Arianna. Of course, Evelyn didn't have time herself for babysitting a teenager right now. That's what they'd paid Carolynn to do all of these years.

"Ari, please," Evelyn said as calmly as she could given the circumstances. "You need to be around us...your loved ones. We all missed you so much. Carolynn is looking forward to seeing you. I want to catch up. You can go to the penthouse another day," Evelyn tried to reason, touching her daughter's leg gently. Arianna tilted her head and looked at her mother through squinted eyes. The look sent a chill down Evelyn's back.

"Please mother. Don't start this bullshit. Concerned mother doesn't fit you well. You don't want to catch up or spend quality time with me...you never have and never will," Arianna hissed, pushing Evelyn's hand off of her knee roughly. Evelyn snatched her hand back as if a venomous snake had bitten her. She pinched the bridge of her nose, trying to quell the throbbing that had suddenly started between her eyes. It was starting again, already—the hate/hate relationship she had with her only child. Evelyn often blamed herself for not bonding with Arianna as a baby. She let out a long breath that seemed to zap all of her energy. Everything seemed to stand still.

"I don't want to be here if my father is not here. I'm over the Hamptons and all of your fake friends. I'm sure you have some kind of party planned for me in there, but I'm not coming. I refuse to be like you mother...a fucking fake, hiding behind money, Botox, and designer clothes... living a big lie. Now either you let me go where I want to go, or you get even more embarrassed when I go in there and tell everyone what a wonderful time, I had in drug rehab," Arianna spat viciously. Evelyn coughed or more like gagged. She felt like her daughter had gut-punched her. She placed her hand on her chest, shocked by her daughter's outburst. She looked over at her only child, and she swore she could see red flames flickering in Arianna's eyes. Pure hatred clouded the girls face. Evelyn's jaw rocked feverishly, and her pulse pounded. Suddenly everything was swirling around her. She cleared her throat like she'd done so many times when preparing to speak to Levi, thinking, Arianna had grown to be just like her father. Evelyn knew she couldn't let Arianna ruin what she had spent years building—the lie that was their life.

"Arianna, I have tried and tried. What more do you want me to do? It is not my fault that your father is not here. I asked him to be here, and he chose to attend a business meeting..." Evelyn started, steeling herself for more cruelty from Arianna. Arianna's face lit blood red, her eyebrows folded into a scowl.

"No! Shut up!" Arianna screamed. "You probably ran him off like you always do. I don't know how he stayed married to you after all of these years with all of your nagging and complaining. Matter of fact, I do know. He stayed with you because of me! It's my fault that my poor father has to endure life with a bitch like you!" Arianna continued with her vituperative tirade. She yanked on the door handle, as the car had started moving through the open gate up the pathway to the house. The driver slammed on the breaks in response. Evelyn's body jerked forward then back, and her head slammed into the headrest. Her heart began pounding even harder, and her head throbbed.

"Oh, my God! Arianna!" Evelyn screamed, wincing, and holding the back of her head. The car had screeched to a halt, and Arianna scrambled out of the door. There was nothing Evelyn could do now.

"Ari! Wait!" Evelyn hung her head out of the door and screamed. It was too late. Visibly shaken, Evelyn decided against running after her daughter. There was, but so much she could take. She knew that Arianna was serious when she said she would tell everyone she was not in Europe; but in a rehab. Someplace deep inside, what all of her friends thought was more important than forcing her daughter to enjoy the lavish party she had prepared.

"Everything alright, Mrs. E?" their driver asked. Evelyn was terribly embarrassed and equally as flustered. "You want me to go after her?" he asked, peering at Evelyn through the rearview mirror.

"I'm fine. She's a teenager," Evelyn replied, trying to seem lighthearted about the incident, but not able to control her voice shaking. "Take me up to the house and come back for her. Take her wherever she wants to go. If she wants to go to the city, let her go to the city," Evelyn croaked out instructions to the driver, her voice finally shedding the false cheeriness she tried on; instead, her words came out laced with pain and anger. It was better than Arianna blowing the whistle on Evelyn's lies.

Once in front of the house, Evelyn climbed from the

car. She steeled herself for the questions and shocked looks she knew she'd face when she stepped inside of her home. Evelyn immediately began constructing more lies in her head. She had become so good at it now that it took her no time to think of what she'd tell her friends about Arianna's whereabouts. Evelyn exhaled a windstorm before she turned the doorknob to her home. It was the first time she had acknowledged that she was losing the battle on all fronts, but she'd made it up in her mind that it wouldn't be for long.

Chapter Three
Shelby's Bratty Ways

"What are we going to do today?" Shelby whined, twisting the end of her silky, blonde hair around her pointer finger. "I am bored, Levi. All you want to do is read articles about the stock market on your dumb computer," Shelby pouted; her long, slender legs crossed Indian-style as she perched on the end of the king-sized hotel suite bed. Levi looked up from his iPad a little annoyed by her whiney, nasally voice. Sometimes the age difference between them annoyed him. He quickly dismissed any ill feelings when he looked at Shelby's perfect, new, store-bought double D cup breast peeking out of her pink, Italian lace La Perla bra. Her neatly shaven vagina winking at him didn't hurt either. Levi placed his computer down next to him on the bed and flashed his winning smile. His blood ran hot in his veins. Shelby brought out the animal in him. This was exactly why he couldn't stay mad at Shelby for long.

"Come here and tell your big poppa what you want to do. Shop? Go out to dinner? Buy a new car? A new boat maybe? Or how about just come over here and fuck me really good like I like it…" Levi replied with a dirty giggle while he rubbed his crotch lasciviously. He didn't care if he seemed like a lecherous old man.

At fifty-seven years old, Levi's taste in women had changed; he liked them younger and younger. Levi felt deserving of the most beautiful, young women around. It was how he was raised. He'd always been like the prince of New York, women at his fingertips and disposal. Levi kept himself in good physical shape thanks to Ravi, his personal trainer and but for the salt and pepper hair on his head, Levi thought he could still pass for about forty-five. He could also keep up with the best of the young men. His wealth was a factor that kept him one of the hottest commodities on the market as well.

Levi eyed Shelby hungrily. Just looking at the twenty-three-year-old beauty kept Levi harder than any Viagra ever could. Levi had known Shelby since she was ten years old and he'd always thought she was extraordinarily beautiful even as a little girl. This year when Evelyn had urged him to hire Shelby as his assistant as a favor to Diane, Evelyn's best friend, Levi didn't hesitate. His intentions weren't to sleep with his wife's best friend's daughter, but things had gradually ended up there. Shelby was undeniably sexy, with her perfect hourglass shape and Scandinavian features. She was the complete opposite of Evelyn, which piqued Levi's interest from the start. Shelby was blond, and Evelyn was brunette. Shelby was aggressive and a constant challenge. Evelyn tried too hard to please Levi, even becoming a pushover most times. Over the course of their marriage, Evelyn had lost her own identity and most of her natural beauty. Shelby was striking, but her best feature was that she commanded respect and had a strong personality. She'd graduated cum laude from Columbia and had ambitions of one day starting her own clothing line.

Evelyn had long since lost her ambition and became

satisfied with just being a wife and a mother. Levi had chosen Evelyn as his wife because at the time she was a lot like Shelby. In 1989, when they'd met, Levi had been struck by the fact that Evelyn, although a model; was different than the vacuous, overly accommodating, too pretty for their own good usual model/actress types he'd met on the elite social scene in New York. At the time, Evelyn had interesting opinions on world issues and had shared intelligent commentary on everything they'd talked about. She used plain English, her words smart and direct, not pretending to be overly educated to impress him. Levi was overjoyed to learn she could actually hold an intelligent conversation on just about anything and that it seemed to come naturally. Evelyn had treated him as her equal and not like she should've been a fan of his. He was more than impressed; in fact, he was bowled over. But as soon as they were married, Evelyn had changed. She'd become what she thought Levi wanted her to be.

Evelyn became enmeshed in the world of the wealthy and abandoned her own career. She never talked to Levi about anything other than home décor or soirees after they married. Evelyn was obsessed with getting pregnant while Levi wasn't interested in having children. She'd turned into just what Levi had spent his entire life trying to run from—a replica of his mother. Levi secretly despised his mother. He'd grown up watching his father walk over his mother like the proverbial doormat. There were many nights as a child, Levi crept to his parent's wing of their mansion and heard his parents arguing or on most nights, his mother weeping. When he grew into a man, he vowed he would get a strong woman, who had her own mind and would give him a challenge. Levi thought Evelyn was the woman, turns out; she was weak and over accommodating just like his mother had been for as long as he could remember.

Levi quickly grew bored with his marriage to Evelyn. But after their daughter was born, he wouldn't leave. He took to entertaining himself with other women. He'd even purposely gotten himself caught a few times thinking that would spark something in Evelyn, make her stand up to him, finally challenge him, but nothing. Evelyn took whatever he dished out. She had relegated herself to just living to please him, and it turned him further away from her.

Shelby coming to work for Levi at his investment company was like having a breath of fresh air waft through the office. She always spoke confidently, and although she was the spoiled brat daughter of Diane and Miles Frankel, she had carved out her own identity. Shelby was smart and equally beautiful. Levi loved her mind and her confidence, both of which overshadowed her looks. When Levi began to get to know Shelby as a woman, he secretly admired her zest for life. Levi wished he could bottle it up and give it to Evelyn to drink like some magic potion that would bring his wife back. He still loved Evelyn, but he had grown out of her. Evelyn hadn't evolved enough for Levi.

After his first under-the-radar sexual encounter with Shelby, Levi was all in. Not only was she a challenge for him because she had sass and didn't bow to his every whim, but Shelby had also given Levi a series of mind-shattering blowjobs that were like nothing he'd ever experienced—and a man as wealthy and strikingly handsome as Levi had been around. He'd enjoyed many explosive escapades' in his day, none of which touched Shelby's skills. Levi was so blown he thought he was

31

falling in love with the girl. There was only one problem; he was married to her mother's best friend, a fact that never seemed to bother Shelby.

Shelby smiled as she watched Levi stroke himself now. She didn't mind entertaining herself with any of the things Levi had just rambled off. She loved to shop, go out to dinner, and most of all; lately, she loved to fuck Levi. She sidled over to him. "How about we do all of the above?" She giggled, letting her bleached blond hair fall around her face seductively. Her icy blue eyes mesmerized him. "Whatever you want," Levi drawled as Shelby straddled him and lowered her head towards his manhood, trailing her tongue down his chest and stomach. "Anything for you," he grunted as she finally reached her destination and took him into her mouth. She moved her head up and down like her life depended on it. The small things, like this, was what made Levi keep Shelby around. Evelyn had never taken him to these places. Never. She was way too conservative in the bedroom for Levi's appetite. "Ahhh," Levi gasped, closing his eyes letting Shelby take him to ecstasy. He didn't have a care in the world. His wife and daughter never even crossed his mind, although they had both left messages on his cell phone.

A few hours later, Levi was roused from him sex induced coma by his cell phone vibrating on the hotel nightstand. He mindlessly reached over and picked up the buzzing nuisance.

"Hello," Levi huffed into the mouthpiece, his eyes still half shut. "Hello?" he grumbled when he got no response. Levi could hear someone breathing on the other end of the phone. His eyes popped open when he finally heard a voice. Levi felt a rush of heat come over his body as the caller spoke.

"You're a dead man Levi Epstein!" the gruff, computer disguised voice on the other end growled.

"Hello? Who is this?!" Levi wolfed into the phone fully awake now; his heart was thundering in response.

"You're a dead man! A dead man!" the caller said one last time before disconnecting the call.

Levi snatched the phone away from his ear and peered at the screen frantically. The last call read UNKNOWN. Unnerved, Levi sat up in the bed and scrubbed his hands over his face. He took in a deep breath in an attempt to calm his heart down. He exhaled and looked at his phone one more time as if something had changed. Levi's movement caused Shelby to stir next to him. "What's the matter, honey?" she rasped her voice still filled with sleep. Shelby leaned up on one arm, letting the sheet fall away from her breasts. Levi looked over at her and parted a halfhearted smile. His bottom lip quivered with nerves. "Nothing. Go back to sleep. Business call from overseas that's all," Levi fabricated on the spot. "Oh," Shelby huffed, yanking the sheet back over her. She wasted no time turning back over to return to her beauty rest. Levi stood up from the bed and walked into the suite's huge luxury bathroom. He flicked on the lights above the sink and stared at himself in the large mirror hanging over the black marble-topped double sinks. He could see worry flickering in his own eyes. Levi had no idea of who the caller was, but the possibilities could've been endless. The thought caused a shiver to run the length of his spine. Levi had finally met his match, and even a man as powerful as he was could sometimes get in over his head. "What now?" he whispered to himself. "What now?"

Chapter Four
Time to Play

Evelyn let out a high-pitched scream as Max hammered into her pelvis. "Oh, God!" Evelyn belted out as she felt herself reaching climax. Evelyn had never had such an earth-shattering experience before she started seeing Max. Max leaned up a little and balanced his weight on one hand. With the other hand, he swiped coil, sweat-drenched locks of his long, dirty blonde hair from his face. "Is that good for you, sweetheart? Is it the best?" Max panted, his thick Venezuelan accent making him seem like he'd just walked out of sexy, hunk Heaven. "Oh! Oh! Oh!" Evelyn screamed as her body quaked all over. Max smiled, and then it was his turn.

"I guess that was good for you?" Max wolfed, satisfied as he looked down into Evelyn's smiling face.

"Oh, Max, you have no idea," Evelyn panted as her body began to relax. Max eased from between her legs and flopped next to her on the bed.

"I've needed that all week. I couldn't' wait to sneak away from all of the crap I have going on," Evelyn wolfed, still reeling from the explosive orgasm. Max laughed. "Glad I could be a' help," his accent making his words sound heavy. He turned on his side and stared at Evelyn's facial profile. He reached over and moved a cluster of sweat-drenched hair strands from her forehead. Evelyn placed her hand over his halting his movement. She inhaled deeply and brought his hand to her lips. She closed her eyes and kissed the top of his hand as she clutched it close to her face.

"You are so sweet," Max commented, his accent always causing him to add an A where it didn't belong. His voice and the accent made Evelyn's heart flutter.

"No. You are so sweet, and you have no idea how much I appreciate you," Evelyn told him with sincerity. She meant every word. Her affair with Max had come just in time. Time with him had been the one thing that had saved Evelyn from going off the deep end when she'd found out that Levi was sleeping with Shelby—a betrayal that had cut so deep Evelyn had contemplated divorce for the first time. Max had changed her mind. As soon as she met him, Evelyn decided Max would help her even the score with Levi. After all, she counted their meeting as fate anyway.

Evelyn had been storming through the lobby of the Upper East Side building that housed the Epstein penthouse when she ran smack dab into Max—literally. "Oh, my God! I'm so sorry!" Evelyn had exclaimed when she realized she had sent a cup of hot black coffee all over the stranger's white shirt.

"Please. Let me pay for your shirt. I...I can buy you ten new shirts," Evelyn rambled, as she used her bare hand and tried to wipe the coffee off of the completely ruined shirt. The man had grabbed her hands, stopped her, and smiled at her. His smile made Evelyn pause, and she had no choice but to stare into his eyes. Evelyn felt something inside of her move...like when she'd first met Levi at fashion week all of those years ago.

"It's ok. This shirt is old," he had comforted, flashing a gorgeous smile.

Well at least let me buy you another cup of coffee," Evelyn blushed; fine beads of sweat had begun rolling down her back. No other man had ever made her flush like that.

"This was already my second a' cup of coffee," he replied winking. "It is ok. Maybe I needed to throw out this old shirt. It doesn't even go with my eyes," he joked, his accent making it all the more amusing. They both burst out laughing.

"I am Maxmillion Vega," he introduced himself, extending his hand towards Evelyn. "My friends call me Max." He was perfect. Perfect skin. Perfect teeth. Perfect eyes. Perfect hair. Most of all, perfect timing.

"Evelyn...um...Evelyn Epstein," she replied sheepishly, as she wiped her wet coffee-stained hand on her skirt and accepted his invitation for a handshake. Her head was swirling with all sorts of thoughts. She had a lot going on at the time, but for just one minute, it had all stopped. Time seemed to stand still in Max's presence.

"I like that name. Evelyn. Pretty name...pretty lady," he complimented, flashing the most gorgeous smile Evelyn had ever seen. Looking at his beautiful green eyes, dirty blonde, shoulder-length hair, and perfect facial bone structure made Evelyn blush again. She knew he was much younger than she was, but he'd made her feel tingly inside like a schoolgirl. She hadn't been called pretty in years.

"Where are you from...I mean...the accent?" Evelyn asked, still wearing a goofy, coy smile.

"I am from Venezuela," he told her. Evelyn was intrigued. Venezuela was one of the places she and Levi hadn't traveled to in the years they spent jet setting. It was however on her to-do list. "Wow…I've always wanted to visit Venezuela," Evelyn said honestly, smiling at Max again. She still couldn't believe how easy it was to meet a gorgeous man like that.

It was the beginning of an hour-long conversation. Evelyn had agreed to walk up the street and re-buy coffee for Max. That first impromptu date led to their next meeting three days later. It was an instant sexual attraction. Evelyn had ditched her driver, and they'd ended up at the Parker Meridian hotel. Once inside the room, their attraction was animalistic. Evelyn hadn't had sex in close to seven months, and she damn near attacked Max. She forced her mouth on top of his, and their tongues did a wicked dance with one another. Max hoisted up her skirt and fingered her hot box. Evelyn gasped at his touch. They kissed passionately until they finally stumbled over to the bed. When Max entered her, Evelyn let the worries of the world fall away from her mind. Max had taken her to places she'd been dying to go for years. Something inside of her sparked anew, and she knew it wouldn't be the last time she would see Max. Evelyn had fucked Max like he was the last man on earth because that was exactly how she'd felt.

In the months following their first date, Evelyn and Max's agreement became a two-sided sort of "friends with benefits" deal. Evelyn helped Max pay his bills; she paid his living expenses and bought him expensive clothes. In return, he gave her the attention she craved, hot sex, and the satisfaction of knowing she could play Levi's cheating game just as well, if not better, than he did. Evelyn felt a sense of overwhelming power, knowing she was spending her husband's money on another man.

Max had told Evelyn he was a struggling part-time male print ad model and that when he made it big, he'd pay her back every dime of the money she spent on him. It wouldn't be a small feat because Evelyn spared no expense on her new boy toy. Evelyn didn't care about the money, the way she saw things Max helped her regain a long-lost sex life, and more importantly, he assisted her with evening the score with Levi. It was a win, win situation for both of them. At least, that is what Evelyn thought. She was happier than she'd been in a long while. But yet again, her happiness depended on the feelings of another person.

"Where are you going?" Max asked, as he watched Evelyn climb out of bed. He wasn't expecting her to be able to move a muscle after their hot lovemaking session. Evelyn smiled. She loved that Max made her feel wanted.

"I have to go back to the Hamptons. My friend Diane is expecting me at her annual all-white affair this evening. If I don't show up inquiring minds will want to know what happened to me," Evelyn explained disappointedly. She walked back over and stroked Max's long hair. "I wish I could stay with your forever," she lamented. He pulled her back on top of him.

"You can do a' whatever you want. C'mon stay longer with me?" he said, making his face like a sad puppy dog. Evelyn smiled. She had never felt so wanted in her entire life. Max gave her purpose these days.

"I wish I could stay longer. This happens to be one night I just can't miss. It'll be interesting, to say the least," she said vaguely, breaking off her words. Evelyn hadn't seen Diane or Shelby since she'd discovered Levi and Shelby's affair. Evelyn was anxious to see how things would play out at the event. She also didn't want to miss it and make all of the Hampton's elite think she was at home burying her head in shame because her husband had a much younger, more attractive, new arm candy.

"What does that a' mean? You can't miss it because…" Max asked seriously, looking Evelyn in the eyes. She pushed herself up off of him. Evelyn grabbed the hotel robe from the end of the bed and wrapped her body with it. She walked over to the lounge chair and flopped down. "Max, I've never really told you everything about me. Of course, you know I am married and to whom, but my life…it's…it's complicated," Evelyn said gravely, her eyes downcast. Max had his head propped up on one hand, and his muscular chest and six-pack abs were on display.

"So, tell me," he urged. "Your husband…he has a lot of a' money no? What does he do for a living?" Max inquired further. Evelyn ran her hands through her hair. She didn't know how much she should be telling her lover, but she knew she felt so close to Max that she wanted to pour her heart out about Levi, Arianna…everything.

"He runs his own investment company. Epstein Trading. He is the investment guru to the stars," Evelyn replied hesitantly. She shook her head like she'd already said too much, especially given what she knew was going on with Levi right now.

"Wow. He sounds like a powerful a' guy," Max replied, sitting up further in the bed. He was interested now. "Big investment banker. Nothing like a' me. A struggling model," he quipped. He had quickly realized that he couldn't seem too interested or it might scare Evelyn out of talking about her husband.

"No. Not a banker, a trader, like a fund manager. And believe me, you're better off than he is on any day," Evelyn shot back. She exhaled and slipped into her pants. As she put on her clothing, she could feel the heat of Max's gaze on her. Evelyn could remember when Levi watched her with love in his eyes like that. She hated the fact that everything she did nowadays she related back to Levi and how things used to be with them. Evelyn needed to clear her head for sure. Maybe therapy. She shook her head side to side in an attempt to pull herself together. She whirled around, wearing a fake smile.

"I have to go. Are you alright for money? I have something for you," Evelyn asked and told Max in one breath, her words rushed. She picked up her purse from the occasional table. She began digging in her purse for the gift she'd gotten for Max before they'd met up the night before. It was just like any other time. She wanted to give Max anything he asked for, not because she had to, but because she wanted to experience how it felt to spend Levi's money on her lover like Levi had done over and over for years. Max sucked his teeth and rolled onto his back.

"I don't want to a' keep taking things from you, Evelyn. I really like you, just for you," Max admonished.

"If he can do it, I can do it too," Evelyn replied mindlessly. She immediately regretted the words as soon as they left her mouth. She could see the look on Max's face and tell she'd let too much of her emotions fly. "Max, I didn't mean it that way," Evelyn tried. But Max had already hopped out of bed and headed into the bathroom. He slammed the door behind him. Evelyn flinched at the sound. Evelyn felt hot all over with anxiety. She couldn't afford for Max to be mad at her now. He was her only outlet. Levi and Arianna both hated her...not Max too. That would be too much to bear.

"Max! Please don't be mad. I'm sorry. You know that I really enjoy our time together. I didn't mean it that way," she called from the other side of the door.

"I guess you can leave you're a' payment on the nightstand if that is a' what I mean to you. Like a male prostitute!" Max called back.

"I'm sorry. I really didn't mean it that way. Please come out and speak to me. Please, I can't have you mad at me too," Evelyn pleaded, hammering her fist on the door. Max slowly opened the door. They locked eyes. "I want to know everything about you, Evelyn. Your life, your kid, your marriage, even your husband. I will no longer sleep with a stranger," Max demanded, grabbing her roughly and forcing his tongue between her lips. After a long passionate kiss, Evelyn melted against him. "I will tell you everything. Just don't ever leave me," she whispered desperately.

Chapter Five
The Good Life

*A*rianna had spent an entire night at her parent's penthouse alone. Everything inside was different…redecorated. Arianna was sure that had been her mother's doing. Trying to rid the place of Arianna's past drug use was probably what her mother had told herself while she had the place totally made over. The unfamiliar surroundings had made Arianna depressed. She didn't know why she'd gone there to be alone when she knew that she really craved to be around her family. That night, Arianna had toyed with the idea of calling her sponsor from the rehab and speaking about how she felt. She'd decided against it. It would make her look weak; she had reasoned. The loneliness had gotten to be too much to bear. Arianna had decided she wouldn't spend another night like that.

Now, Arianna pushed her way to the front of the line outside of Torrid nightclub—one of her old haunts from her party scene days. It seemed like ages now. She was confident the bouncers would recognize her as the VIP that she once was and allow her to skip the long line that wrapped around the building out front. Maybe confident was a strong word to use…Arianna decided she was more hopeful the bouncers would recognize her than confident. "Excuse me. Excuse me," Arianna huffed as she jostled her way through clusters of bodies. She surely wasn't used to that. Waiting in line with the general public wasn't something she did back when she lived that life. Six months away was like years in the party world. Things changed so fast; Arianna felt like she was in a foreign land. She was so lost in thought she ran right into someone. "Um...sorry...um, excuse..." Arianna mumbled. "Hey, bitch! Watch where you're going! There is a goddamn line you know!" a girl with purple hair, black lipstick and safety pins for earrings screamed at Arianna drawing angry murmurs from other impatient partygoers on the line.

Arianna ambled forward, stumbling a little bit. Her eyes were wide like a lost puppy. She realized she had never visited the club unless she had been high out of her mind. She never knew what the crowd was really like there. Arianna immediately hung her head and walked faster through the crowd. Her mind raced, leveling with the fact that she'd never been to any of the clubs in New York City sober. Everything was always a blur, even the potential dangers of being out there. Being clean was opening her eyes to an entirely different world that she wasn't used to. When she finally reached the front of the line, the six-foot, seven-inch-tall, three-hundred-and-fifty-pound bouncer at the door was not familiar to her. He looked like a mountain compared to Arianna. There was nothing small on the man at all. He was surely going to be an obstacle. Arianna wasn't used to obstacles. Things usually came easy to her. "Shit," she mumbled, her pulse quickening as she really took a good look at the bouncer. She pulled out her cell phone and dialed the number she'd been calling incessantly for the past twenty-four hours. Maybe he will answer this time. I hope he answers this time.

She said to herself as she listened. Her shoulders slumped. She got the same result she'd gotten all day and night. No answer.

"Hey! You! Lost girl! This looks like the place for you to stand to make a call?!" the bouncer barked, his double chin and dark, close-set eyes making him resemble a Gorilla. He was scary as hell. Arianna blinked rapidly, her heart thundering in her chest. This was her chance. It was be brave now or never. She swallowed the lump that had formed at the back of her throat. A strong desire was propelling her forward with imaginary courage.

"Um…do you know…um…can you get Cosmo for me? Can you tell him, Ari, …um…Arianna, is outside to see him?" Arianna stammered, her tongue seemingly not cooperating with her brain. Arianna hated feeling like a scared little girl. Being sober fucking sucked. Had she been high she would've had the confidence to march right up to that fucking monstrous bouncer and demand that she be let into the club. Not now. Arianna had nothing in her system that could bring her old Arianna back. She hated it.

The bouncer scrunched his eyebrows and flexed his neck. He looked down at Arianna like she was crazy. "I look like an errand boy to you? Get the hell outta' the way of my line. You wanna get inside to see Cosmo…you get to the back of the line like everybody else," the bouncer spat dismissing her. Doesn't he know who I am?! I am Arianna Epstein…daughter of…! Arianna screamed inside of her head. She could feel tears welling up at the backs of her eyes. Having major tantrums was what she was used to whenever she didn't get her way.

Arianna didn't know what to say next. She stepped closer to the door, her teeth chattering. She tried to dial the number again, but her hands were trembling too badly. She needed a hit…a pill…anything to take the fucking edge off. Now that she was out of the safety of the rehab, all of her drug desires were back. The cravings had returned the minute she walked into her parent's penthouse. That was the reason she'd come out tonight, to fight the urges. Yea, right. Who was she fooling? She'd come out to see the person she'd longed for the entire time she'd been gone.

"What you can't hear?!" the bouncer barked, moving his large Jabba the Hut body towards her menacingly. "I said this isn't no place for you to be standing to make no damn calls! Get your ass to the back of the line or get the hell out of here! Period!" Arianna jumped, but she wasn't giving up. She bit down into her bottom lip, swallowed hard, and stepped up again.

"I really, really need to see Cosmo. If you just give him the message, you'll see, he'll let me inside. Please…please, it's an emergency," Arianna pleaded, clasping her hands together like she was about to pray. It wasn't in her nature to beg or plead. All of her life she'd gotten what she wanted, even on the party scene. She was used to getting her way with everyone, but she figured the temper tantrums she usually threw or the rude way she spoke to her parents wasn't going to work with this guy. "Pretty please," she added for good measure. It was clear to the bouncer that this little nuisance wasn't going to give up. He didn't have time to keep arguing with her either. The bouncer exhaled a windstorm of breath and rolled his beady eyes. "Alright, alright. Just hold up because I see you aren't gonna give up and you are fucking up the order of my line here," he relented. He let three more people through the blue "Do Not Cross" barricade, and then he looked at Arianna one more time and turned around towards the nightclub doors. She stood trembling, the uncertainty killing her inside.

"Aye JoJo run inside and tell Cosmo a little hot piece of ass is out here to see him. I'm not letting her inside unless he gives the ok. Names Ari or some shit like that," the bouncer yelled over his shoulder. Arianna's shoulders slumped with relief. Cosmo was still hanging at his usual spot, which was good. The bouncer turned back towards her, his face twisted as if he smelled something stink.

"You must really need to see Cosmo. Don't look like his usual type. You look too clean for the likes of Cosmo," the bouncer commented, eyeing Arianna up and down. She wasn't really in nightclub attire; she assumed that's what the bouncer meant by Cosmo's "usual type." Had he changed his type that fast? Did that mean Cosmo had moved on without her? Arianna's mind raced a mile a minute.

"I did you a favor, now get out of the way. Stand to the side until I see if he wants to be bothered with your ass," the bouncer instructed, using his Gorilla hands to push her aside. "Next!" he screamed, calling forward the next three people in the line. Eager club-goers rushed towards Arianna, causing her to stumble back a few steps. The world was so strange to her without drugs in her system. Arianna didn't know how she would survive without medicating herself.

Arianna shifted her weight from one foot to the other as she waited for her boyfriend Cosmo to either come outside or give the beefy guards the word to let her inside. The last time she'd seen Cosmo, he'd given her a fix in exchange for her American Express black card. All she remembered of that night was coming into consciousness in the back of an ambulance surrounded by chaos and screaming EMTs. A day later, she was released from the hospital to her parents who'd driven her straight to the Passages Rehabilitation center. She'd been forcefully dragged inside, but after a lot of futile kicking, spitting, screaming and crying; Arianna had still been signed in involuntarily. Which Arianna believed was all her mother's doing. Being at the rehab, she'd been cut off from the world… and Cosmo.

"Yo, Cosmo said to come inside," the bouncer grumbled, interrupting Arianna's thoughts. I knew he would be excited to see me! She smiled, and her insides began churning with fear and excitement. "I told you he'd let me in," she admonished, rolling her eyes at the bouncer. He just shook his head at her. She stepped past the patrons on the line with her nose in the air like she was an A-list celebrity. Suddenly, she had that old, entitled, feeling back. The old Arianna wasn't far away from the reaches of her mind at all. This is how I'm supposed to be treated.

Once inside, the smell of marijuana immediately shot straight up Arianna's nostrils. She swallowed hard as her mouth filled with saliva like a hungry dog hearing the dinner bell. Arianna could hear her substance abuse counselor, Ms. Heddy's voice ringing in her head, "When you go home any exposure to drugs or the old scene you were used to will cause you to relapse. It will be too dangerous for you if you go back to your old habits. Find new friends and new places to hang out."

Arianna was glad the blaring music filled her ears now. It made it that much easier to shake off the warnings ringing in her head. What did those counselors know about her in just four short months? Arianna felt like she could control her desires to get high if she wanted to. She told herself she was a big girl, and she could handle herself. She didn't want to get high right now; she just wanted to see her man who she'd missed for the past four months. Arianna hadn't been able to reach out to Cosmo while she was away in rehab with all of the restrictions placed on the telephones and with telephone calls being monitored. Arianna was sure it was her bitch of a mother who'd added Cosmo's name to Arianna's "no contact list." She often wondered if Cosmo had ever tried to find her, possibly visit her while she was away. Be strong when you see him. He is going to be so happy to see you. You'll see. Arianna pep talked herself as she waded through swaying club patrons.

As Arianna navigated the crowd and reached the back of the club, she spotted him right away. How could she miss him? It was like they were kindred spirits. Made for one another. Besides, Cosmo was unmistakable; even in a club packed with people. He always wore the same close-fitting black t-shirts that exposed his muscular chest and huge biceps no matter what the weather. His deep olive-colored skin, dark brown, doe eyes, and obligatory moussed hair gave away his Jersey Shore Italian upbringing. Those same features also made him the bad boy that all of the girls loved. Cosmo was a wanna-be mafia henchman that hung around real Italian mafia capos and did their flunky work. He was also a two-bit drug dealer that preyed on young women with money—his specialty being homemade methamphetamine, the street name--crank. He had introduced Arianna to the drug when she was just sixteen.

Seeing Cosmo after all of this time, Arianna's heartbeat sped up until it was hammering against her chest bone. She felt hot all over her body, and sweat beads popped up on her forehead seemingly out of nowhere. Cosmo had spotted her as well. He squinted his eyes and put his drink down on the bar. Arianna let a goofy smile spread across her face as she rushed towards him. Cosmo didn't move, but for the frown that caused his thick eyebrows to come together and dip so low between his eyes, they almost touched the bridge of his nose. Arianna was oblivious to his reaction to her. All she knew was that she was seeing her man.

"Hey Cos," Arianna sang, her arms outstretched ready to embrace him for a hug. Cosmo twisted his lips and his facial expression. He moved to dodge contact with Arianna. She felt a flash of pain flash through her heart. Cosmo had always welcomed her with nothing but open arms.

"Well if it isn't poor little miss rich bitch. I thought my eyes were fucking with me. Outta' jail I see…looking good too…good and rich," Cosmo replied bitterly. Arianna dropped her arms at her side. She didn't know how to react to Cosmo's treatment. "And the first person you come see is me? Wonder why?" He continued cruelly. Arianna's throat tightened. Didn't he miss her? She had missed him terribly. All she thought about in rehab was Cosmo. No matter what the counselors said about drug dealers, she never attributed any of those horrible things to Cosmo. In her assessment, Cosmo was different, nothing like the rest. It didn't matter that he got her hooked on the worst drug to hit the streets.

"Cos…I missed you so much. You are the first person I thought of when I woke up each morning and the last person when I went to bed. I have missed you so, so much," Arianna sang, her voice rising and falling with emotion. Her underarms itched with sweat. Her mouth became cotton ball dry. Arianna really wanted to run into Cosmo and hug him as tight as she could. Something told her it wasn't a good idea, so she settled for standing her distance, pleading with him.

It wasn't long before reality hit. Arianna saw a slim, dirty blonde, with deadpan eyes wearing a skirt so short it looked like a loincloth, move close to Cosmo and kiss him on the neck. The scary girl looked at Arianna and licked her tongue down the side of Cosmo's face. Oh, my God! He moved on. He is with someone else! Arianna screamed inside her head. Arianna felt a sharp pain flash through her stomach. She swallowed hard and tapped her foot. She suddenly felt an overwhelming urge to urinate. She shifted back and forth on her feet as she watched the girl enjoy what was hers. Arianna swallowed hard, willing herself not to scream and cry. Cosmo spread a sly smile across his face, pulling the girl closer to him.

"What do you want lil' girl? As you can see, I'm busy," Cosmo said to Arianna, chuckling at her like she was a big joke. Arianna opened her mouth to speak, but the words wouldn't come. Then Cosmo turned towards the gaunt girl hanging on his neck and planted a deep tongue kiss on the girl. Arianna closed her eyes for a long second. She felt like her legs would just give out. Arianna hadn't felt a sinking, deep, pain of disappointment like that since her father missed one of her birthday parties one year.

"Cos, you know it wasn't my fault. My mother…I didn't want to go…I would've called you…please don't do this to me," Arianna began on the brink of tears, her voice cracking some more. Cosmo emitted a shrill laugh that interrupted her and sent her words tumbling back down her throat like hard marbles. Arianna could feel tears burning at the backs of her eye sockets.

She didn't know how much longer she could hold it back. Please God, don't let me cry.

"Cos just give me a minute to explain," she croaked. She was moving and didn't even realize it. Arianna wasn't used to this type of rejection. She was anxious. She wanted to get high, so badly now she could actually taste it on her tongue.

"Look, little girl. I've moved on...you can crawl back to your daddy and mommy and leave me alone. I don't have time for you anymore," Cosmo snapped irritably. He grabbed the blonde closer to him for emphasis. "I have no time for the rich girl chronicles anymore. As you can see, there's a new sheriff in town. I only got you in the club tonight to see if it was really you. Shit, I thought your rich daddy had whisked you away to some remote paradise somewhere," he continued tauntingly. "Other than that, I have nothing to really say." Cosmo was laying it on thick. He'd always known how to get inside of Arianna's head. She would do just about anything to get him back at this point.

"Let me just talk to you alone," Arianna pleaded, touching his arm boldly. The ugly, skeleton of a girl moved in front of Cosmo and blocked him with her gaunt body. Arianna's jaw rocked as she snatched her hand back.

"Aye! You can't fucking hear?! He said he doesn't have anything to say to you! Now get the fuck away from my man before I get angry! I don't have much sense when I get angry!" the girl hissed, jutting a pale, bony finger towards Arianna's face. A pang of fear shot through Arianna's stomach, but she held her ground. "Cosmo...just give me a minute," Arianna said persistently. Cosmo kind of liked this attention.

"It's alright, Kris. I'm not going anywhere," Cosmo comforted the girl, grabbing her around her waist to move her out of Arianna's face.

Arianna backed down for a minute. She could feel tears stinging at the backs of her eyes. She was trying to think fast, desperate for Cosmo's affection.

"Cosmo...I'm back. Me. Ari, your girl. Remember, you promised me that we would always be together. Remember. The money. The shopping. Remember. Everything we had together. All of the things we shared. I just want to be with you...I don't care if she's here. I just want things to be like before. I need you Cos," Arianna droned on pathetically. She was shameless with her begging, but the truth of the matter was that when she was with Cosmo, he had been the only person that made her feel like she really existed. Her parents had always gone about their busy lives like she was just an added burden. They would throw money at her with the hopes that they could buy her whatever would take the place of their presence. Cosmo had paid her the attention she had craved, especially when she had things like money and credit cards to offer him. All Arianna wanted was to feel loved again...needed again.

Cosmo looked at her now with intense interest all of a sudden. It was like Arianna had said the magic buzzwords—money, shopping, things...one of those had piqued his interest. Cosmo had almost forgotten how easy it had been to get large sums of money from Arianna during their time together. Cosmo moved his new love interest aside. He looked at Arianna, a devious line streaking his brow. Cosmo was quickly reminded of how easy it had been back then to get Arianna to hand over thousands of dollars to him. Arianna knew she had gotten his attention now. The yearning she felt inside grew bigger. The anticipation was making her sway on her feet involuntarily. I knew he would remember what we had! I will always be his number one! Arianna said to herself, a satisfied look on her face.

"Kris baby, let me just talk to her for a minute. It's the only way I'm gonna get rid of her," Cosmo whispered to the girl loud enough for Arianna to hear. Arianna smiled and bounced on her toes. She didn't care what excuse Cosmo used to get rid of Kris. Arianna longed for his attention…his touch. Arianna's hand shook uncontrollably like Cosmo was a hit of some powerful drug that she was dying to get high on. She felt like if she could just get a few minutes alone with him, he'd be hers again. Kris sucked her teeth and folded her arms across her chest. She eyed Arianna evilly. Something inside of Arianna felt vindicated, powerful even. Arianna smirked at Kris as Cosmo walked towards her. Who was Kris anyway? She didn't understand what Arianna and Cosmo had. Their love had been powerful. It had been Arianna's life back then. It wasn't so long ago that she had all of Cosmo's love and attention. Arianna was hell-bent on getting that back, no matter how long it took.

Cosmo brushed past Arianna now, and not without Kris' stony gaze on them both. "Follow me," Cosmo huffed as he stalked towards the back of the club. He knew damn well he couldn't speak to Arianna with Kris so close by. Not the way he wanted to anyway. Arianna turned and gave Kris a squinty-eyed grin. Her facial expression saying, "I have him now bitch." Arianna wanted to stick her tongue out too, but she figured that would be way too juvenile. Kris rolled her eyes and flipped Arianna the bird. Arianna could see Kris's nostrils flaring. Arianna fell in step behind Cosmo, finally following him into the men's bathroom. She felt extra special. She would be alone with her man…the way it was supposed to be. Once inside, Cosmo didn't give Arianna a chance to say a word. He knew exactly what to do. He grabbed her by her arm, turned her towards him, and forced his tongue between her lips. "Mmmm," Arianna moaned, a bit caught off guard. It didn't take Arianna long to return his efforts. She melted against him. She kissed him ravenously. Oh, how she had missed him during her time in rehab. "Mmmm," she moaned some more as tears leaked out of the sides of her eyes. They were definitely tears of joy. Cosmo groped her body as he pressed his body into hers roughly. Arianna wanted him so badly. She wanted to feel him inside of her. She slid her hand down to his crotch and felt his manhood against her hand. It was just as she remembered it… just right. She could barely breathe now. They didn't even care that someone had entered the bathroom as they feasted on one another for another ten minutes. Arianna was all in now.

"I missed you," Cosmo said cunningly in between kisses. It was like he wasn't even the same mean, disdainful person from a few minutes ago out in the club. Arianna held onto him like he was about to run away. She wanted to savor every moment with him. She looked into his face. His slick, dark hair and deep dark eyes were so sexy. Arianna's heart rate sped up.

"I missed you too, Cos. I'm sorry I had to leave and go away like that. I didn't know what happened to me. They said I almost died, so they got all spooked out. I tried to fight it. I really did…I would've never left you like that for one minute. Then my mother…" Arianna rambled, finally coming up for air. She had finally let the tears fall in streams down her face. She was so happy to be back in Cosmo's embrace that she never wanted to leave. "I would've never left you like that. I just want things to be the way they used to be. Please, I need you. I want you so bad," Arianna whined pleadingly. Cosmo knew he had her now. He liked seeing her like this. At his mercy was right where he wanted Arianna to be. It was so easy to get her there again. Kris had been a much harder nut to crack.

"Shhh," Cosmo put his finger to Arianna's lips. He didn't need to hear all about the past. He was interested in what she could do for him now. "So, what's up? You said you got your money back and everything?" He wasted no time getting to the real point. Arianna didn't care either. Too blinded to see through his scheming manipulation. She shook her head vigorously in the affirmative.

"Yes. My access has been unblocked. I called my father while he was away on his business trip and he gave me back all my access...to every account. I can get anything I want right now. Just like before. Of course, my bitch of a mother doesn't know anything," Arianna told Cosmo, nervously wringing her hands together. Arianna tried to grab him again. She wanted to feel his touch again. Cosmo was too busy pacing now. She knew that meant his mind was racing, calculating. Whatever it took to keep him around, she would do it. "If you get rid of her it'll be just like it used to be for us Cos," Arianna said, her tone serious.

"Can you get your hands on like ten thousand dollars?" Cosmo came straight out and asked. He acted as if she hadn't even mentioned getting rid of Kris. Arianna's eyes popped wide, and goosebumps came upon her arms, given the fact that she'd just lied to him about having access to her trust fund and her father's accounts like before. Her heartbeat sped up. Arianna shifted her weight from one foot to the other. She had to think quickly. There was no way she could let Cosmo slip through her fingers now. Not after she had just gotten him back where she wanted him. A lie popped into her mind so fast it was like second nature.

"Probably tomorrow. Not tonight," Arianna replied uncomfortably. "I can get it first thing tomorrow. Are you going to see me tomorrow? Without Kris?"

"Alright, yeah, yeah. You need to come to the loft and see me tomorrow. Bring the cash...all of it," Cosmo said sternly. "I'll make sure she's not there when you come. But you gotta' bring the cash. I'm depending on you now." He touched her chin gently and urged her to look him in the eyes. "I want to be able to trust you again, so don't fuck this up. If you ever leave me like you did before...I don't know what I'll do with myself," he said, puppy dog eyes and all.

"What does this mean, Cos? I mean...for us. You know...like are we...what...are we," Arianna stammered, blinking rapidly. Cosmo grabbed her head and pulled it into his and kissed her deeply again. The kiss was so forceful it left Arianna breathless. Huge bat-sized butterflies flitted through her stomach.

"It means you never stopped being mine," Cosmo replied, looking into her eyes seriously. Something inside of Arianna seemed to melt. Cosmo was the only person who had ever made her feel like that. It was like they were the only two people that existed in the world when she was with him.

"Here this is for you...on the house. A welcome home gift," Cosmo said, shoving a foil-wrapped bundle into Arianna's hand. Arianna stumbled back a few steps clutching the package. She knew right away what it was. She felt like throwing up right there on the spot. Blood rushed to her head and the room starting swimming around her. Immediately an intense throbbing started at her temples. It was too much to handle. Having Cosmo back. Being exposed to drugs. It was a lot to handle.

"Cos...I'm...I...I'm clean. I can't...I don't...," Arianna stammered, the vein at her temple pulsing fiercely. It was her first test being clean and sober. Just like that, she had drugs at her disposal again. It hadn't even taken her any effort to get it. Arianna clutched the little bundle so hard the center of her hand began to sting. She wanted to give it back to him, but her hand would not unfurl to release it. It was a gift from her one and only love...a gift from Cosmo. She couldn't bring herself to let it go although she knew what it could do to her. Cosmo walked into her and kissed her again. This made Arianna clutch the bundle even harder.

"Just take it. If you don't want it...then throw it away. But consider it a gift from me. I always want to do nice things for you. Besides...one little hit like that isn't gonna do shit to someone like you. You used to do at least three or four of those a day, remember. Those were the good days...me, you, and that shit right there," Cosmo said smoothly, knowing exactly what he was doing to her inside. "I don't even give chicks out there gifts like that. But see, you're different. You're someone that will always have first place in my heart." He pecked Arianna on the lips again and left her standing there. Cosmo was right. Arianna did remember when it was only the two of them. She remembered doing so many bundles in one day that she would start feeling like she could conquer anything when she was high. She remembered feeling better about not having her parents around like she had secretly wanted her entire childhood. She remembered feeling loved by Cosmo most because he cared enough to give her drugs and a place to get high. Arianna could remember everything about how she felt when she was high. In her mind, there seemed to be way more benefits to being high than sober. It was like Cosmo said…that little package was light work for someone like her. She could probably take it and still be clean. Arianna's hand stayed curled into a fist around the foil bundle. Suddenly the room was spinning around her, and she felt faint.

Chapter Six
The Hamptons

*D*iane and Miles Frankel's Hampton home was a magnificent sprawling mini-mansion that sat directly adjacent to the shore. It was one of the biggest homes in the Hamptons. Sand dunes surrounded the grounds, which from street view, made the house look suspended in the air. Evelyn had visited the home hundreds of times, but today she was breaking out in a sweat as she approached. It definitely wasn't the same feeling she'd gotten when she visited with Levi. Evelyn squeezed Max's hand as her Bentley eased towards the Frankel's circular driveway. Max looked at her. His eyes seemed to sparkle against the crisp whiteness of his newly purchased Dolce and Gabbana shirt. Evelyn felt warm inside under his gaze. She wondered then if she was really falling in love with Max. She lowered her eyes so he wouldn't see her blushing.

"Are you as a' nervous as I am?" Max asked, his tone more serious than Evelyn had ever heard it. Evelyn chuckled, trying hard to stave down her own nerves. She knew this was the boldest thing she'd ever done in all the years she'd been married…but she also knew it was necessary.

"Don't be silly. I'm not nervous at all. If I was going

to be all shaky about this, I wouldn't have invited you, now would I?" Evelyn said, lying through her teeth. "I am looking forward to the reactions. Especially with you know who's," she continued. She leaned over and kissed Max on the lips—a bold display of affection that he wasn't expecting. Max flinched as he caught the eye of Evelyn's driver watching them. The driver had seemed surprised and a bit angry at Evelyn's bold conquest. Evelyn saw him watching, and she knew his loyalties lied with Levi, but she didn't care. She needed to do this…for her.

Evelyn had decided to bring Max along to the party after they'd had a long talk at the hotel. She knew full well all of her friends would be there. The same friends that knew she was married to Levi for the past twenty years. Evelyn was tired of Levi always having the upper hand, and she knew he'd be there and so would Shelby. With Max by her side, Evelyn felt powerful, bold, and vengeful. The car finally stopped in front of the house. The Frankel's hired help rushed over and opened the door of the Bentley to allow Evelyn and Max to exit. Evelyn extended her long, slender legs and grabbed the awaiting servant's hand. Max waved off the help and climbed out by himself. He looked around, enamored. So, this is how the rich and shameless live? Wonder what crooked investor lives here? He thought looking around like a little kid in a huge candy store. Evelyn gave him a halfhearted smile. She could see that he was impressed, but scared to death. Her eyes told him she was also nervous, but playing it as cool as she could. "Here goes nothing," she said with a chortle that said she was really about to fall apart inside. Max didn't know how he felt about this anymore, either.

Evelyn smoothed down the bottom half of the shocking

white Herve' Leger bandage dress she wore. The dress fit her perfectly and made her look at least ten years younger, especially the way it pushed up her D cup breasts. Max did the same with his white, Gucci slacks. Evelyn nervously forged ahead into her friend's house, Max hot on her heels.

"Mrs. Evelyn Epstein and guest!" a white-gloved butler announced his voice reverberating off the walls inside the grand foyer of the home. Diane Frankel seemed to appear like magic. It was as if she just materialized out of the walls. Diane glided over to Evelyn, her wispy, white, Nicole Miller dress flowing around her like fake angel's wings. Evelyn was immediately relieved she didn't purchase that same dress.

"Evelyn!" Diane sang, rushing into Evelyn for a hug. "You look fabulous! So slim and trim as usual," Diane continued her phony song and dance, air-kissing Evelyn on each of her cheeks. The two women had done this same song and dance so many times it was like they'd memorized the steps and the words to the song like some sort of pledge.

"You look amazing too darling," Evelyn returned in the same fake singsong, finishing up their familiar ritual. Evelyn gave Diane the once over. Evelyn could tell by the plastic, semi-permanent grin on Diane's face that she'd had a fresh round of Botox, probably that morning if Evelyn knew Diane as well as she thought she did. Diane's carrot-colored hair was freshly dyed, and her makeup painted on in layers as usual. Diane was often told she looked like an older version of actress Angelina Jolie. A compliment Diane often repeated with pride. Evelyn begged to differ. Diane clearly wore her age like a badge. And unfortunately for her, there was no amount of plastic surgery could help. They'd been friends for almost twenty years, and the competitiveness between the two got deeper and deeper each year. Diane resented the fact that Evelyn had been a top model and still had unmistakable beauty. Evelyn resented the fact that, although Diane wasn't as beautiful, Diane's husband Miles treated her like a rare and precious stone. There had never been any rumblings about Miles having affairs. In fact, all of the Hampton elite often remarked at how much of a faithful, dedicated man Miles was.

Max stood off to the side, watching the perfunctory exchange between the women. For the first time, an ominous feeling crept into his gut as Evelyn acted as if he wasn't standing there. He fiddled with the stitching inside of his pants pockets, wishing he'd declined the invitation. It was a bold move to say the least.

"Well, the party is outback as usual. You know the drill, Evelyn. Eat, drink, and be merry. There is plenty of the finest food and libation. We always want our guests to feel at home! Enjoy! Enjoy!" Diane sang some more. Evelyn smiled and raised an eyebrow. She was waiting for Diane to ask. Evelyn started counting down in her head. Five, four, three, two...I knew it! Evelyn said in her head as Diane turned back towards her. "Oh yes, before I forget, I thought I heard them announce you with a guest. Is Levi outside?" Diane asked, her eyes darting over to where Max was standing looking into space with his hands shoved deep into the pockets of his pants. Diane looked back at Evelyn, then one more time over at Max. Evelyn knew that Diane had figured out that Max was with her, but wanted to hear it from Evelyn's mouth.

"Oh, no. Levi didn't bother to come with me. I think he said he would be hereafter his so-called business trip. I think he'll show up whenever Shelby gets here," Evelyn said snidely. Diane's fake smile started to fade. "Oh?" Diane said, her eyebrows furrowed a bit. She blinked rapidly as she tried to understand what Evelyn was getting at.

"I am here with a good friend of mine; his name is Max," Evelyn announced smugly with an air of audacity. She let a huge smile spread across her face. She felt the heat of satisfaction wash over her. "Max! Oh, Max, come let me introduce you to one of my best friends, Diane Frankel," Evelyn said, smiling from ear to ear while waving Max to her side. Max's eyes popped open like he'd been splashed with cold water. Moving like Frankenstein, Max stepped close to Evelyn. The fine blonde hair on his arms stood straight up, and his heart thundered. It was awkward to say the least. Evelyn grabbed his arm proudly and squeezed his bulging bicep. "Yes, this is my Maxy," Evelyn beamed. Diane's mouth hung open. She didn't even realize that her perfectly drawn on pink lips were agape.

"Hello madam, I am Maxmillion Vega. It is very nice to make your acquaintance," Max introduced himself; his accent seemingly more pronounced than Evelyn had ever heard it. He grabbed Diane's hand and kissed the top of it. Max wanted to push her lips closed, but he didn't dare. With his hair down and the first three buttons on his shirt left open, Max was a male bombshell in a Fabio kind of way. Diane couldn't close her mouth or hide her shock. She felt a bit lightheaded. When Max released her hand, she let it drop to her side stiffly. Diane fanned her face with her other hand. She had to admit; her legs felt a little weak after Max's touch. "Well, I...I...I mean, it's very nice to meet you, Max. Very nice to meet you indeed," Diane gasped like Max had taken the air out of her lungs. Evelyn

63

smirked, a blanket of vindication settling over her. Levi Epstein is not the only one who can play these games. I can still snag a hunk myself. I'll be the talk of the town for another reason now. Evelyn was thinking as she watched her friend come completely undone over Max.

"It's not polite to gawk, Diane," Evelyn chortled. She grabbed Max's hand boldly and headed towards the party leaving Diane standing with what Evelyn was sure was a pair of soaking wet panties and her cheeks red as strawberries.

The Frankels' party scene was simply stunning. Evelyn and Max stood at the doors leading to the party for a few minutes to take in the elaborate, beautifully decorated estate. There was no doubt that the Frankels had tried to outdo every other Hamptons party that summer. "Wow," Max said to Evelyn. Now he found it hard to close his mouth. "Yes, yes, I know…each year she tries to outdo the year before. I'm not at all surprised by all of this," Evelyn replied, a hint of jealousy apparent in her tone. As usual, Diane had spared no expense on her annual all-white affair. It seemed like she'd gone a bit more overboard this time. Evelyn knew Diane was probably trying to outdo another of their friends who'd had a summer soiree a few weeks prior. This year's theme at the Frankel's was Asian fusion. There were round, white linen, Chinese lanterns hanging in clusters on invisible wire around the huge backyard. There were enough lanterns to cast a heavenly glow around the entire place. The poolside was adorned with glowing, square candles with Asian inscriptions on them. The candles glinted off of the crystal blue water in the pool. All white calla lilies floated in the pool's glistening water. Wind chimes hung from the large oak at the left of the yard. The sound was soothing. There was a band, but they played Asian music, low, soothing, and just loud enough to be considered a party. Diane had also spared no expense when it came to the food. There were several food stations—including a seafood station with huge lobsters on ice. A gorgeous ice sculpture of a dragon sat like a museum piece in the middle of the chafing stations. There were servers walking around with silver trays of vegetable spring rolls, sweet and sour shrimp, crab wontons, and lobster hors d'oeuvres just to name a few. All of the patio and pool furniture was covered in crisp, freshly starched white linen. The entire place seemed to glow. "Wow, this is a big a' deal," Max whispered to Evelyn as he took it all in. It was far more than he was used to. The things rich people spent money on never ceased to amaze him. He could definitely see Evelyn doing something just like this. Especially the way she spent money on him when they'd gone shopping.

"I told you so. There is nothing she wouldn't do to impress others. We better grab a few drinks and get wasted now. We'll need it. Trust me." Evelyn whispered back to Max as she fielded the stares they received from some very familiar faces. Evelyn flashed a plastic smile and waved to a few of the Hampton elite. She was soaking up the attention. She blew fake hand kisses to others, but she never stopped to have any face time with any of them like she usually did. "Are all of these people rich?" Max asked, astonished at how many people were there hob-knobbing. He was trying to remember faces and find out names if he could. Max's interest was piqued.

"Some are rich, some lie, and most are like Levi, living off the fat of the land," Evelyn answered furtively. Max seemed to contemplate what Evelyn was saying. Living off the fat of the land? He thought. He would have to follow up on that later. He grabbed a Martini off of one of the beautifully decorated tables and downed it. Evelyn took her time sipping her drink. She would need a constant distraction. She was just counting down the time until her husband arrived, and things got very interesting.

It didn't take long before Evelyn and Max had become the topic of the party. Hushed murmurs and sideways glances lingered around the Frankel estate. All aimed at Evelyn and her "friend." Evelyn knew they were talking...that was the point. Diane's husband, Miles refused to come over and speak to Evelyn after Diane had whispered in his ear that Evelyn had come with a "friend" and not Levi. When Miles turned his head abruptly, Evelyn was staring right at him. She knew she was the topic of their secret conversation. Diane had cracked a fake smile at Evelyn and then chastised Miles for looking at Evelyn and Max too quickly. Evelyn had smiled back and waved, but Miles just pushed his lips out and turned his head like he hadn't seen Evelyn. Miles had even told Diane she should have put Evelyn out of the party. Everyone knew about Levi's affairs, but the nerve of Evelyn! Miles had been Levi's friend by default for many years. Evelyn was out of line in Mile's eyes. How dare she bring her little boy toy to their home!

It seemed like Evelyn and Max had been at the party for an eternity. Evelyn had quickly grown tired of the stares, snickers, and fake smiles. She looked at her watch impatiently. When was Levi going to show up? Just as Evelyn picked up her fourth drink, she heard what she'd been waiting for all night.

"Ms. Shelby Frankel!" the butler announced loudly. Evelyn's heart jerked in her chest. Everyone seemed to turn towards the door at once. Smiles and almost cheers abounded. Not for Evelyn. Her reaction was different. Evelyn almost dropped her drink when she heard the butler announce Shelby's arrival. She leaned into Max, her voice rising and falling. "This is the whore who has Levi's attention now," Evelyn grunted, jealousy apparent. Max seemed surprised that Levi's mistress would be at the same party. "Uh…she is a friend of yours?" Max asked incredulously. "Not a friend of mine…per se. She is my best friend's daughter," Evelyn corrected sharply. Max and Evelyn watched as Shelby popped into the party amid ohs and ahs and obligatory "hello darlings." Shelby seemed to glide and glow at the same time. There was no doubt about her natural beauty. Evelyn watched with rapt attention. Max didn't want to seem too interested, but he had to agree that Shelby was definitely noticeable.

"Don't worry. She is not as a' beautiful as you," Max quickly came back sweetly. With arched eyebrows, he took in Shelby's beauty. She looked adorable in a silk, one-piece, strapless shorts jumper. Her long, tanned legs, were accented by a pair, of sparkly, rhinestone covered, Christian Louboutin D'orsays. Her hair was pulled back in a sophisticated chignon with a few loose strands that were purposely left untamed to fall around the sides of her oval-shaped face. Shelby worked the room like a top rate socialite. She learned how to schmooze and be fake from the best—her mother. She kissed a few people, gave out hugs freely, and garnered lots of attention. Evelyn watched Max as he watched Shelby. Envy built up inside of Evelyn like a pressure-filled pipe. I'll be damned! Evelyn moved closer to Max and dug her nails into his arm as she pulled him close to her face.

"You must think she's beautiful too," Evelyn hissed is Max's ear. The drinks she'd had easing her reticence. She suddenly regretted bringing Max along. Who was she fooling? Even being with a man as gorgeous as Max couldn't take away the insecurity, she felt about her husband's mistress. Evelyn felt like crying and screaming. Shelby was young, popular, and gorgeous. All of the things Evelyn felt that she was not anymore. She suddenly regretted bringing Max along. What if he fell for Shelby too?

"Never," Max assured, breaking Evelyn's train of thought. "I only have eyes for you. She is a coquette. I can a' tell what type of girl she is and trust me, that does a' not interest me. Only a real a' woman like you can keep me interested," Max finished up, touching Evelyn gently on her waist. She exhaled and put her hand on top of his. She felt slightly better.

"I'm sorry for talking to you like that…" Evelyn began, but her words were cut short.

"Mr. Levi Epstein!" the butler announced. It felt like someone had rung a bell in Evelyn's ear. She flopped down on one of the white chairs, her legs suddenly too weak to stand. She looked at Max, and he looked at her, both exchanging knowingly nervous glances. This was it. The moment she'd been waiting for. Evelyn steeled herself for what was to come. She also felt a flash of satisfaction, fear, and anger all at the same time. Evelyn picked up her newly filled Martini glass and downed it. No more nursing drinks. It was showtime. Evelyn made a snide chuckle. "How stupid can they be?" she snapped, looking at her Rolex. "Not even five minutes apart," she grumbled, shaking her head. It was very apparent that Shelby and Levi had tried to appear as if they'd arrived separately. Max darted his eyes around the room nervously. "Keep your composure," Evelyn told him. She needed Max to be on his A-game. She needed him to be better than Levi right now. "Levi doesn't like to be bested at his own game," Evelyn followed up. She was sure there would be a showdown once Levi realized what she'd done. It was the moment she was waiting for too. Having two men fighting over her was the confidence booster Evelyn needed. She tapped her foot under the table. It was all she could do to stave down her wiry, nervous system.

Evelyn watched her husband come through the doorway like he owned the night. Levi still had the presence of a world leader and the allure of a king. He waved and smiled. He was still strikingly handsome, even at his age. Evelyn felt something inside her chest tighten. She still loved Levi, and she couldn't help but admit that to herself silently. All eyes were on Levi. His hair was neatly trimmed; he wore an all-white purple label Ralph Lauren button-up that Evelyn had given him as a gift for one of the many occasions they exchanged thoughtless, obligatory gifts. She couldn't even remember now if it had been a birthday, anniversary, or some other special day that didn't mean shit in their marriage anymore. Levis had his muscular, toned legs on display under his white Armani shorts. Evelyn swallowed hard as Levi shook hands with Miles, kissed Diane and greeted a few of their other friends. His attention was soon directed towards his wife and her friend. Some of the partygoers could hardly control their excitement, watching things unfold. Levi smiled, laughed even. He had to show his friends that it didn't matter that Evelyn came there with a stud like Max. What mattered most to Levi was that he would not be beaten at his own game. Levi's jaw rocked as he took long, confident strides through the beautifully decorated estate. Finally, after prolonged greetings and handshakes, Levi walked over to Evelyn. He approached the table with a giant's presence. He smiled.

"Evelyn," Levi nodded, with his eyes set on Max. He folded his arms across his chest.

"Levi," Evelyn returned, dryly. Her hands trembled fiercely. She didn't know if it was nerves or the rush of revenge. Evelyn tilted her head as if to say, "can I help you?" Levi and Evelyn looked at one another for a long minute.

"I told you I'd make it in time," Levi said flatly, breaking the eerie silence that had settled between them. Max shifted under Levi's gaze helplessly. He didn't know whether to stand up and greet his nemesis or remain seated. Max felt vulnerable, like a sitting duck.

"You did. Glad to see you and Shelby could pull yourselves away from work to make it," Evelyn said sarcastically, lifting her Martini glass to her lips. She needed something as a distraction. Max stood up. He'd seen Levi's hands curl into fists. That was signal enough for Max to be on guard. There was no telling what Levi was thinking.

"Excuse me," Max said, attempting to walk away. He was clearly uncomfortable.

"Gotta' go to the little boys' room, do we?" Levi hissed, sizing Max up and down. Max returned Levi's eye-fuck showing no signs of the fear that was banging around his chest. Max chuckled. He wasn't going to show Levi that he was scared. The two men exchanged a long, heat-filled gaze.

"I'll leave you to talk to a' your wife. Seems to me you have a lot to talk about," Max replied, still eyeing Levi boldly before walking away. Evelyn's cheeks were flushed, to say the least. She could feel her foundation cracking under the heat. Levi bit into his bottom lip. His nostrils flared, and suddenly he felt the tension rise in his neck. "You thought bringing someone here was wise Evelyn? You thought that would make you look strong?" Levi growled. It was the open-door Evelyn had been waiting for. With the alcohol swilling in her system and Levi's indignation setting her temper ablaze, Evelyn squinted her eyes into dashes.

It was as if time had stood still. All of the activities of the party seemed to freeze, and everyone stared at Evelyn and Levi like they were watching a movie. Evelyn stood up to meet her husband face to face. It was the first time in years she'd stood up to him and stopped pretending that she didn't know what was going on. Her gaze was filled with the fire of redemption.

"You have some nerve questioning me! Did you think you were the only one who could do it? You think I don't know about you and her?! You think I am that stupid, Levi. Well, as you can see, two can play your game. I guess I'm not the rundown old wretch you thought I was huh, Levi? I guess you got your answer tonight!" Evelyn gritted and attempted to walk away. Levi bit into the side of his cheek until he could taste his own blood. He hated to be embarrassed. He knew everyone was watching them. Evelyn of all people knew this about him.

Levi grabbed her arm roughly. "I don't care what you know. You will not disrespect me in public. You have the nerve to bring your little boy around our friends to embarrass me! You've made a deadly mistake!" he hissed, his grip digging into Evelyn's arm. Evelyn was too riled up to feel the pain. She wasn't backing down this time. There would be no running to her room to cry. Not today. She was standing her ground.

"What do you care? Did you care when you started fucking Shelby, who happens to be my best friend's daughter!" Evelyn boomed, just as the band changed the song playing. Her voice carried through the party as if she'd screamed into a microphone. Loud groans from some of the partygoers echoed throughout the expansive yard. Evelyn finally wrestled her arm away from Levi just as Shelby dropped her glass and ran into her parent's house. The damage had been done. Everything had been revealed now. Grumbles and groans spread amongst the partygoers like the plague. Diane's face was as red as a cooked lobster. Her lips were pursed.

Diane stomped over to Evelyn, and in a knee-jerk reaction, she slapped Evelyn in the face. Evelyn held her cheek in shock. "In my home, Evelyn! You bring your soap opera drama to my home! How dare you!" Diane spat.

"No! How dare your whore of a daughter!" Evelyn retorted, her face stinging.

"Get out of my house! Get out!" Diane screeched, the veins in her neck bulging. She was mortified by her friend's outbursts. Diane spun around on her heels to see who had been watching this nightmarish scene.

"Oh, I most certainly will! But not before you know the truth!" Evelyn spat as she dug into her bag and took out a manila envelope. "I think the next step is to have these all over the media. I wonder how Shelby's new business venture will fare then! I wonder if she would look like the innocent, young, beauty then!" Evelyn hissed as she shoved the envelope containing the photos of Shelby and Levi into Diane's chest so hard that Diane stumbled backward clutching her chest like she'd been shot. Evelyn could see a few people clasping their chest and with hands over their mouth.

"Now, dear friend! We'll see who wins or loses this time!" Evelyn finished. She stomped away and stormed through the foyer towards the front door. Just as she made it to the door, Max rounded the corner from the restroom. He whipped his head around because Evelyn was moving so fast. Max changed his course, following her lead.

"Evelyn?! Wait?! Is everything ok?" he called out as he ran after her. Max didn't know what the hell was going on, but he could just imagine. "Evelyn!" he called out again.

"Ms. Arianna Epstein!" the butler shouted just as Evelyn and Max made it to the door. Evelyn almost fainted when she saw her daughter. Evelyn suddenly had the urge to throw up. She hadn't been expecting Arianna to really show up there. This was all too much. Evelyn would've never had Max accompany her if she knew her daughter was going to be there. The last thing Evelyn wanted was to drive a bigger wedge between herself and her daughter. Evelyn's cheeks flamed over as Arianna looked from her mother to Max and back at her mother again. Max squeezed Evelyn's shoulder. A show of his support. Evelyn wanted to slap his hand away but couldn't move. She stared at her daughter unable to speak.

"Where are you going?" Arianna asked rudely. She looked at Max like he was a monster then back at her mother for clarity. "Mom, what is going on?" Arianna asked, quickly folding her arms in front of her. Evelyn's face turned dark. She was sick of Arianna and Levi.

"Ask your father. You'd prefer to speak to him over me anyway," Evelyn hissed as she headed out of the house and towards her awaiting car. Max tried to follow, but he couldn't help but look back at Arianna.

"She has a kid too?" Max mumbled under his breath, realizing there may be some very important things he had yet to find out about Evelyn Epstein. How had he missed that? He wondered as he followed her like he'd been doing for months now.

Chapter Seven
The FBI

A high-tech Nikon camera clicked in rapid succession capturing each high-class partygoer as they exited the Frankel estate. The extended lens sat outside of the slightly cracked car window and caught close up shots of both men and women, and no one was spared. "Did you get him yet?" Special Agent Rick Assisi asked his counterpart who was adjusting the focus on the camera's lens. More clicking, adjusting, more clicking.

"Well, if the information Vargas, oops I meant, Maxmillion Vega, called in was correct then we got our man and a few of the other players we've been watching," Special Agent Arnold Kemp replied as he lowered the camera onto his lap and began unscrewing the extended lens. Both men laughed at their running joke.

"Shit, I've been working for the FBI for fifteen years, and I never got to go undercover and be the boy toy of a rich bitch," Kemp snorted. "Can I get an assignment where a rich former model takes me to St. Tropez? And buys me Gucci, Prada, Fendi…"

"Hey, let's face it Vargas looks the part. I can't see you passing for a Venezuelan model," Assisi taunted, rubbing

Kemp's pale, balding head. Kemp slapped his hand away and shot him an evil look. "Well…it's the truth."

"What other information did Vargas provide on the call?" Kemp changed the subject. He wasn't much in the mood for being teased today. They'd been sitting in that cramped car for hours while the spoiled rich bastards sipped Moet and munched on caviar.

"Vargas said old lady, Epstein told him that our guy runs his own trading company to the stars. That he is known amongst Hollywood's, who's who for bringing in eighteen to twenty percent return on investments, but she thinks there is something fishy about her husband's business dealings. Told Vargas, or Vega as she knows him, that she found some documents that her husband had doctored to show profits when she knew his company had suffered losses during the stock market crash. She knows he has been putting money and assets in her name, but he doesn't know that she knows. She seems to think that Levi Epstein collects more and more so-called investment money, but he is faking the returns. So, looks like Levi Epstein continues to collect millions from his clients under the guise that their money is growing. It was a Ponzi scheme at its fucking best. From the returns we received on the grand jury subpoenas to the banks, Mr. Epstein has been living tax, fucking free, off of his clients' money. One hundred percent loss to those poor unsuspecting bastards," Assisi relayed.
Kemp whistled and shook his head. "Another fucking Bernie Madoff, huh? Robbing Peter to pay Paul."

"I think he might have Madoff beat. Levi Epstein has swindled more than the sixty-five billion Madoff got away with," Assisi replied, gravely. They both seemed to contemplate the brevity of what they were saying.

"And to think…he'll be going down all because his wife wanted to even the score. I guess I have to agree with the saying it's cheaper to keep her. Happy wife means a happy life," Kemp chortled as they pulled out and began trailing the Bentley that held their undercover agent.

The day after his alter ego caused a dust-up between Evelyn and Levi, Marcellos Vargas rushed through New York's Penn Station, his dirty blonde hair blowing behind him like a cape of confidence. He was dressed differently than he had been the past few months he'd been undercover. No European cut jeans, close-fitting shirts or pointed toe hard bottom shoes today. Instead, Vargas donned a grungy, worn, black motorcycle jacket, a pair of loose, dirty blue jeans and his black riding boots. No Venezuelan model today. He looked at his watch and sucked his teeth. He was late for his meeting with his two case agents, Assisi and Kemp.

Vargas had overslept after spending another night holed up with Evelyn Epstein. He had comforted her the entire night after the spectacle at her friend's party in the Hamptons. Evelyn had begged him to stay with her a little while longer. How could he have said no? Evelyn thought he belonged to her given the fact that she believed he was her model boy toy. Vargas was only able to break away after he'd told her he had a model booking that he couldn't miss. It had even taken him more than an hour to convince her he had to go. Vargas had rushed to his government-commissioned apartment and changed, picked up his evidence, and rushed to his meeting. He was sure he would take a bunch of jawing from the guys for being late. It was part of the job.

Finally, Vargas reached the small pizzeria inside the bustling station and ambled to the back. It had been there meeting spots since the inception of the case. Agents Assisi and Kemp were already there, digging into greasy slices of the best pizza in the city. Vargas caught their attention as he approached. The digs began immediately, full mouths and all.

"Ay, if it isn't lover boy Maxmillion Vega himself," Assisi called out sardonically, his Italian Mafioso bravado coming through. He wiped his mouth with the back of his hand like a caveman and threw his half-eaten slice onto the greasy paper like he'd just lost his appetite.

"You finally grace us with your presence? I guess you couldn't pull yourself away from that cougar that attacked you," Kemp said, making his own dig. Kemp and Assisi both laughed. Vargas rolled his eyes. It was going to be one of those kinds of meetings. Bullshit, bullshit, and then a little bit of work.

"Alright guys, enough. I'm sorry, I'm late. Damn, I couldn't just leave her like that," Vargas replied, his words totally devoid of any Venezuelan accent. He had left Max behind just like that. "You think it's easy playing Maxmillion Vega the Venezuelan pretty boy model when I really want to be home riding my Harley and picking up young hotties on a highway somewhere," Vargas said sagely. Being undercover wasn't as easy as his colleagues thought it was. He resented the fact that they believed he was just living the high life.

"I guess we can give you a pass. I mean, I wouldn't know what it's like to kiss those fake, collagen injected, pillow lips on Mrs. Epstein's face," Assisi joked, frowning like he'd envisioned something repulsive. Vargas just shook his head in disgust. He wanted to curse Assisi out, but he held his composure. He had to get on with the meeting in order to get back to Evelyn.

"I'll have you know she is a very nice lady. And she is attractive for her age. A little plastic surgery, yes…but still pretty damn good looking for a woman over forty," Vargas defended as calmly as he could. Assisi looked at Kemp with a raised eyebrow and then back at Vargas. They were both thinking the same thing. Assisi cleared his throat and shifted uncomfortably in his chair.

"So, to clarify, you ain't sleeping with that broad on the job, right? Assisi leaned in close to the table and asked. Vargas' face flamed over. He balled up his toes in his boot. He smirked. It was all he could do to take the heat off of himself.

"What you think I'm stupid?" he replied, reaching for a slice. "Nothing more than a lot of hot petting and kissing," he lied again. Breaking his eye contact with Assisi, Vargas chewed his pizza. He looked up to find both men staring at him. His eyebrows shot up, forming arches on his face.

"What? C'mon, I think my undercover manual says that's all on the up and up. I have to do what it takes to get all of the information…remember those words. Besides, I spend most of the time with her shopping for expensive shit and going to banks so she can give me cash. All in a day's work, right?" Vargas clarified briskly. Assisi and Kemp seemed to relax a bit. They'd followed Vargas to most of those shopping and bank trips. He had shut both men up. Since the day they'd set Evelyn up to meet Vargas, he'd brought them tons of great evidence against Levi Epstein. They couldn't argue that. Whatever method he was using was working. It had been the only way they'd been able to find out what banks

Levi Epstein used to further his schemes, who his clients were, and more importantly, keep track of his every move without alerting him that he was being investigated. In their years as financial fraud investigators, they'd quickly learned wives and children were the easiest route to a suspect.

"So, give us all the new stuff you have," Kemp said, throwing down his fourth slice of pizza. He leaned back in the chair, his gut struggling against the small buttons on his dress shirt. Vargas pulled a black bag from under the table and sat it next to the pizza box on the table. With a game show host hand gesture, Vargas presented the bag. "That's everything from the past two weeks. I was able to get five more account numbers...the black card, the plum card, and some new start-up bank Epstein is dealing with, Citrix Bank in Fort Lauderdale. I think the manager is in Epstein's pocket. The wife complained about not having enough access since some of the accounts with larger balances were switched over," Vargas relayed between bites.

Assisi picked up the bag and brought it to his lap. He unzipped the top just enough to peek inside. He looked back up at Vargas with wide eyes. "A fucking Rolex and a Hublot in just two weeks?! She bought these outright?" Assisi asked, incredulously. Kemp and Assisi looked at Vargas long and hard. "Either you got a powerful jaw lock, or she's stupid and out of her mind," Assisi finally commented. Vargas knew he had to play it cool. He swiped a lock of hair from his face and shook his head.

"No, I can't take any of the credit. It's not anything special that I'm doing...trust me. Evelyn Epstein just wants to hit her husband where it hurts. In his pockets," Vargas replied, his legs shaking back and forth nervously under the table. That answer seemed to put both case agents at ease again. Vargas hated the fact that these meetings were becoming more and more uncomfortable for him. He wondered if he was really starting to formulate feelings for Evelyn.

"We need to get his computer. Since you were able to convince her to take you to that party in the Hamptons, which got us some great stuff, maybe you can coax her into taking you to whatever home houses his home office...the computer he uses the most. I'm sure there are loads of files, and better still, e-mails. Just like Madoff, these white-collar crooks always, always perpetrate their fraud through the wire. We are close, very close, but we need the whole cigar. Understood," Kemp said, his tone serious. Vargas dropped his half-eaten slice of pizza and reared back in his chair. He scrubbed his hand over his face and leaned into the table with a grave look on his face.

"I will try, but there is no guarantee that she'll pull another stunt like the party. I think she regretted bringing me so close to her life. I mean, getting even is one thing, but it literally blew up in her face. She thinks Levi will come after her, or worse cut her off," Vargas told them.

"I think he knows better than to cut her off. I'm sure Mr. Ponzi Scheme himself knows that his wife has been sniffing around. He knows she has dirt on him. So, we better keep a close eye on her and make sure she doesn't have any untimely death accidents," Assisi warned, raising one eyebrow at Vargas knowingly. They all fell silent. No one had seemed to think about the danger they'd put Evelyn Epstein in when they'd made her an unsuspecting informant against her own husband.

Vargas left his meeting and immediately called Evelyn. "Hey, sweetheart, it's Max. I just a' wanted to check on you," he crooned, Venezuelan accent back in full effect. He smiled when Evelyn told him to meet her back at the Parker Meridian. She made his job way easier than any other undercover assignment he'd ever been on.

Chapter Eight
The City Life

Cosmo's loft was in New York's meatpacking district. It was inside of a swanky, warehouse-style building that had been converted into luxury lofts. The inside of his loft boasted almost 2,000 square feet, and Cosmo had it decked out with gaudy red, black, and white ultra-modern, leather couches and chairs, Zebra print throw rugs and large black and white framed art of various parts of a woman's anatomy. The loft and its trappings were just as arrogant as Cosmo. A lot of the things inside had been purchased with Arianna's American Express card while they had been dating.

Arianna had been at the loft for two days now. It had been easier than she'd thought it would be to get her father to advance her the money, which, she'd convinced him was to buy new clothes and to get back on her feet. She'd seen both of her parents at the Frankel's party, but it hadn't turned out so well. When her father finally explained to her that her mother had shown up to the Frankel's with her lover, Arianna had felt sick and embarrassed. She was never told about her father's affair with Shelby of course. Arianna was too ashamed to face the partygoers, so she turned right back around and headed towards the city, straight into Cosmo's clutches. The first night, Kris wasn't there. Arianna had had Cosmo all to herself. When Kris showed up the next day, things had been contentious, but only until Cosmo pulled out the drugs. Arianna and Kris were getting along fine, so long as they could get high. Cosmo had found it amusing.

Cosmo stood over Arianna now as she sniffed the first line of a new type of crank, he'd just acquired from his supplier up in Spanish Harlem. Of course, Arianna had agreed to experiment with him in the name of love and money. Cosmo pushed another line of the new strain in front of Arianna and urged her on. He watched her closely, waiting for the reaction his supplier told him he should expect. Arianna sniffed the last line, and the rush went straight to her head. Arianna fell back against the couch at first; her eyes rolled up until the whites were the only parts showing. Cosmo watched intently, waiting patiently. Suddenly, Arianna jumped up out of the chair and began walking fast, in circles around Cosmo's S-shaped glass coffee table. Cosmo jumped at first. Arianna's sudden movement had startled him. He quickly realized she was tweaking on one hundred, just like his supplier had guaranteed. Cosmo smiled evilly, confident that he had bought some good shit. Cosmo slapped his hands together at his accomplishment. He watched Arianna for a few minutes. She was jumping around now, flopping her head side to side like a wild, rave dancer. Thoroughly amused, Cosmo bent over at the waist laughing. "Look, Kris, she's tweaking like a junkie! This shit is supreme! I'm gonna clock a ton on this shit," Cosmo shouted excitedly pointing at Arianna like she was a circus act. She was dripping with sweat just that fast. She had no control over her body. It swayed like she had no bones. She moved like she was in a race for her life. "I gotta' get some more of that shit," Cosmo said thoroughly amused. "Ahahah! Look at her go! Look at the rich bitch go!" Cosmo was satisfied that this would be it. He was sure Arianna would be hooked again, which meant his pockets would be padded again. It had been a very small investment with a huge return in his assessment.

Arianna began going even faster around the table now. They didn't know how she hadn't passed out from exhaustion yet. She was soaked with sweat now. Her cheeks were flaming red, and her nostrils flared. "She better not fuck up my table or I'll have to charge her twenty thousand this time," Cosmo said, laughing even harder. Kris, Cosmo's new love interest, eyed Arianna with contempt. "That's what happens when you get high after being clean for so long," Kris pointed out dryly, rolling her eyes. She had already grown tired of having Arianna around. "She looks like she's about to collapse…must be some powerful shit."

After their first meeting at Torrid, Cosmo had enlisted Kris's help in swindling Arianna out of the money. He'd told Kris his plan to act like he loved the dumb, sheltered rich girl until he got what he wanted. Kris never thought about the fact that Cosmo was doing the same thing to her at one point. Cosmo kept Kris so high, most of the time, Kris didn't think at all. She certainly didn't think about her mother, Deana Shepherd, New York's most popular socialite.

Kris's mother, Deana never missed an A-list event, nor did she ever miss any opportunities to be seen in photos. She had several business ventures, but none brought Deana more attention than being known as the one who'd tell the paparazzi and tabloids everything that was going on inside of those exclusive events. Move over Perez Hilton, Deana Shepherd has you beat. Was Deana's motto. Deana fashioned herself as the pulse of the celebrity gossip world. The one thing Deana didn't have her finger on the pulse of, was her daughter. When Deana divorced from Kris' father, Kristoph Yunger, frontman of Living Dead, a multi-platinum rock band that toured with the likes of Ozzie Osborne, Deana divorced her child as well. Deana just wasn't interested in being a mother after her husband left. Kris lived with her father at first, but she couldn't get along with his new, very young, wife. Kris tried moving back in with Deana, but the two argued incessantly. Kris hated her mother. Deana had never shown her daughter any love or affection from the time she was born. She often told Kris she was just like her father—a future drug addict who'd lose everything to a habit. Kris finally left her mother's house again; this time she began staying here and there with so-called friends. She met Cosmo, and so went her journey down the dark path of drug addiction. Kris often saw her mother on television, but she acted as if she didn't even know Deana, except for the check Deana sent her every month to stay away. Even that had slowed now. Kris often thought about going to one of those big red-carpet events and letting everyone know just who Deana was…a neglectful parent of a drug addict. Most of the time, the only thing that kept Kris from outing her mother was being too high to get going.

"Hey! Sit down already!" Cosmo yelled at Arianna. "Hey! Did you hear me!" Arianna was jumping in place now. There was not a dry spot on her entire body. Her body moved like a rag doll, loose and limp. "Hey! Don't you fucking hear me!" Cosmo yelled again, clapping his hands loudly. Arianna kept moving like she couldn't hear him. He stalked over to her and grabbed her around the waist roughly. "Quit moving!" he shouted in Arianna's ear as if he thought she was deaf. Finally, she stopped moving. Cosmo had to hold her tightly to halt her movement. Arianna's face was as red as a cooked lobster, her hair stuck to her sweat-drenched brow and her eyes were glazed over. Cosmo's eyes grew wide when he really took a good look at her now. It wasn't funny anymore. "Shit," he mumbled under his breath. Arianna looked pale like she would collapse at any minute. He slapped her on the cheeks. "C'mon, you can't twitch all night," he screamed at her, jiggling her chin roughly. After a few slaps, the initial rush began to break, and Arianna could hear Cosmo's voice. Still amused by his handiwork, Cosmo dragged her over to his chocolate brown suede accent chair and plopped her down. Arianna stared straight ahead like a zombie; her eyes stretched to their capacity. Kris and Cosmo watched her for a few minutes, their minds racing in opposite directions for sure. Cosmo walked around…thinking. He knew by the looks of things; he had given Arianna too much of the powerful mix.

"Whoa, that was some powerful shit you gave her, Cos. Let me hit that," Kris said, hungrily. It didn't matter that Arianna looked like she was about to die of exhaustion and could barely control her breathing. Kris was sold. She had never seen crank do that to anyone else and she'd damn sure never experience a superior high even remotely near that. She was jealous that Cosmo had chosen Arianna to test his new product and not her. Cosmo blew a puff of air from his lips in response to Kris's request. He wasn't thinking about getting Kris high, he was thinking about the money he was going to make off the new meth.

"Only that pure, backwoods, trailer park made shit for her. Can't you understand what's going on here? Just reeling her back in until I get what I want from her," Cosmo whispered in Kris's ear. "If your skinny ass take a hit of this shit, your rock star daddy and media whore mommy will be burying you," he followed up, chuckling. That wasn't what she wanted to hear. Kris pushed away from him. She really wanted to claw his eyes out. She scrubbed her hands over her face and pushed her tangled hair back on her head. Kris began pacing in front of Cosmo. She bit down into her bottom lip until she drew blood. She wanted some of those drugs. Her mouth filled with saliva just thinking about the high she'd seen Arianna experience. "C'mon, Cosmo just give me one hit. A small taste. Please," Kris pleaded. "I mean, you did it for her," Kris whined like a baby. She was ready to throw herself on the floor kicking and screaming for some of that drug.

Cosmo's eyes hooded over and within a minute he was in Kris' face. He grabbed her cheeks roughly and squeezed as hard as he could. "I said, fucking no! Stop being a junkie and shut the fuck up while I check on her," Cosmo said dismissively, releasing her face with a forceful shove. Kris went stumbling. He began walking in the direction where Arianna was slumped over.

Kris stomped over to him and got in his face. Her hunger for the drug had given her a false sense of courage. "There's but so much I'm going to take Cosmo! I mean, like, just because I get high doesn't mean I'm going to stand by and watch you fuck her and get her stoned and say nothing about it. I'm supposed to be your girl, not her! You don't even need her money!" Kris shot back, her face turning beet red. Cosmo's hands curled into fists, and he rushed into Kris like a bulldozer. Kris stumbled backwards from the force. "What did you just say to me?" He growled, unclenching his fists and grabbing Kris around her skeletal neck. He lifted her off her feet by the throat, cutting off her air supply. She immediately began gagging. Her feet dangled mercilessly as she tried in vain to get her fingers between Cosmo's grip and her neck.

"Close your fucking mouth! You want her to hear you and mess up our plan?! Huh? You can't get another dime out of your mommy and daddy, except for that bullshit hush money your mother sends, so how do you think I've been keeping you high? Do you think your habit is free? How the fuck you think you have a roof over your dumb head?" Cosmo gritted through clenched teeth as he squeezed Kris's neck mercilessly. Kris clawed at his hand as she gasped for breath under the tight grip he had on her throat. Her efforts were in vain. "Now, if I tell you to go along with a plan…any plan, I don't care if it's for you to get in bed with her and have some girl on girl action, you will fucking do it!" he finished, releasing Kris onto the floor just before she blacked out. Kris landed on the hardwood floor in a heap. She curled up into a fetal position gasping for breath. This was the side of Cosmo she hated to see. The abusive, crazy, side. He was showing it more often now than ever. Tears streamed down her eyes. She was left with the reality that Cosmo was the only person she had right now.

The next morning the sun streaming across her face snapped Arianna out of an almost comatose sleep. She came into consciousness with pain wracking her entire body. The first thing she felt come alive with excruciating "Mmm," she moaned, as she turned her head to the left and tried to move her right arm over her eyes. The pain behind her eye sockets was unbearable. "Ouch," she moaned, her tongue felt lead-heavy. Arianna squinted her eyes, the pain-causing tears to run out the sides of her eyes and pool in her ears. She blinked rapidly, and things started to come into focus. She was on the floor; she could tell that. Her back ached with a pain that she'd never felt before. So did her legs, arms, neck, and rib cage. Arianna swallowed hard; her throat was desert dry. Then she inhaled, trying to get oxygen to her brain so she could think. "Ugh," she grumbled. An acrid, metallic smell shot straight up her nostrils. "Ewe," Arianna said, raising her hand over her lips as the smell threatened to make her throw up. She swallowed the bile that was rising from her stomach into her esophagus. Arianna placed her palms flat on the floor and exerted some effort. She tried to sit up, but the room was spinning, which made her flop right back down. "Owww," she groaned as her head hit the floor. "What the hell is that smell?" Arianna mumbled. Arianna painfully moved her head to the right, and the smell seemed to become more pronounced. "Oh God," she rasped. Finally, Arianna opened her eyes wide enough to see things in full clarity. "Kris?" Arianna groaned, using what strength she had left to sit up this time. Arianna quickly forgot the pain pulsating through her body. She could see the girl lying a few feet from her. Arianna pulled herself up off the floor. When she finally got to her feet, she looked down at Kris, who was lying face down on the floor. Kris's dirty blonde hair was splayed over her head and the floor like a yellow spider web. "Kris? Kris, wake up. Where's Cosmo?" Arianna croaked, pushing at Kris with her foot. "C'mon, Kris. I know you hear me. I need to get out of here," Arianna groaned.

"Don't play hardball; just tell me where Cosmo went. He has my keys and my wallet," Arianna said, panic lacing her words. "Kris! Get up!" Arianna raised her voice as much as her sore throat would let her. Arianna finally bent down and shook Kris roughly. Kris's body was stiff. Arianna used what energy she could muster to push Kris's body over onto her back. "Kris…I know you hear me," Arianna demanded as Kris's head lolled to the side. Arianna finally took a good look at the stiff girl.

"Oh, my God! Kris!!" Arianna screamed, her body starting to shake. Arianna whirled around on the balls of her feet. She could no longer feel the pain pulsating through her body. Her headache was suddenly gone. "Cosmo!! She's bleeding all over!" Arianna whirled around and around. "Mmm! Oh, my God! Oh, my God!" Arianna cried, flailing her hands in front of her. She looked back down at Kris whose lips were dark purple. Kris's mouth hung open, and blood covered her chest. Arianna was frantic. She suddenly had to urinate, and her chest heaved. Arianna touched her own body to make sure she wasn't injured too. She looked down at herself, and there was blood all over the front of her shirt and jeans. "What is going on?!" Arianna cried out loud. Arianna began tugging at her clothes. She felt under her shirt for injuries. She wasn't cut. She wasn't bleeding either. Arianna touched her jeans and brought her bloodied hand up in front of her face covered in wet blood. Arianna bent over and threw up. She fell to her knees and started to crawl away from the dead girl. Arianna made it to the kitchen peninsula and rested her back up against the wall. She couldn't control her breathing. Her heart was galloping in her chest. She looked over at the body again and began to sob. Arianna put her hands up to her head, but that just smeared Kris's blood into her own hair. The room was spinning. The smell. The sight of Kris lying there, stiff and lifeless was all too much. Arianna held onto the hair at either side of her head and emitted a high-pitched scream.

It seemed like an eternity before the police showed up. Arianna sat on Cosmo's couch, hugging herself and rocking back and forth. She couldn't even remember calling 911. The loft was now swarming with uniformed police officers, the crime scene unit, the medical examiner's office, and plain-clothes detectives. They were all moving like busy bees, their movement making Arianna dizzy. She watched as several of them huddled together, whispered, and then looked over at her. Finally, a tall, slender, female detective headed towards where Arianna sat shivering. Arianna eyed the woman tentatively. She reminded Arianna of the lady from Law and Order, and her name escaped Arianna at that moment. The scene all went together like a television episode in Arianna's mind. Girl wakes up covered in dead girl's blood...prime suspect...murderer. Arianna imagined what the headlines would say.

"Arianna, I'm detective Baynor," the Law and Order look-a-like introduced, kneeling down in front of Arianna and extending her hand. Arianna looked at the detective blankly. Detective Baynor was fairly pretty to be a lady cop, Arianna was thinking. She didn't know why she was able to tell that at a time like this, but it was all she could do to keep herself from screaming some more. Detective Baynor finally dropped her hand and exhaled. "Arianna, honey, we're going to need you to tell us what you can remember about what happened?" Detective Baynor said softly, patting Arianna's knee. Arianna lowered her eyes and rocked even harder. A streak of frustration

92

flitted across Detective Baynor's face. She was trying to be patient; Arianna could tell that patience wasn't her strong suit as the detective set her jaw squarely and blew out a windstorm of exasperated breath. "Listen, the only way we can help you is if you help us," Detective Baynor said, finally getting hold of her calmer self. Arianna didn't say a word. She was truly speechless. Her mind was as blank as the day she was born. She couldn't remember even coming to Cosmo's loft days ago.

"Was there any drug use going on here last night?" she asked Arianna. Arianna began to cry and shake her head back and forth. Didn't they know how frustrating it was not to be able to remember anything, even the last time you'd taken a piss?

"You need to tell us the truth. There is a dead girl lying over there, you're covered in what appears to be her blood," Detective Baynor huffed, pointing towards the gang of law enforcement professionals surrounding Kris's body. "The only way we get to the bottom of what happened is if you start talking. I suggest you think long and hard," Detective Baynor chided, her patience finally gone. She came to her feet and hovered over Arianna like a dark cloud about to rain down on her. There would be no more getting down to Arianna's level. In the detective's mind, this girl knew exactly what happened, and she was being difficult. Detective Baynor knew it was important to try to get the girl to say something before she got her mind together enough to ask for a lawyer. In Baynor's experience, these little rich, spoiled types always knew their rights.

"I can't remember anything," Arianna finally rasped through tears. Her voice was barely audible. It was completely gone from all of the screaming. "You wake up covered in blood, as you reported, and you don't remember anything,"

Detective Baynor repeated, her eyebrows furrowed. In a flash of commotion that got Arianna's attention, Cosmo arrived at the loft. Arianna sat up when she saw him. Where has he been all of this time! Her mind screamed. "Cosmo!" Arianna called out as she jumped up from the couch, getting ready to rush towards Cosmo. Arianna's sudden movement startled Detective Baynor, causing her to whirl around on the balls of her feet. Detective Baynor glanced towards Cosmo and back at Arianna. There was no way these two were going to get anywhere near one another to make up a story. Baynor knew better.

"Arianna, sit down," Detective Baynor castigated, trying to use her body to block Arianna's view of Cosmo. Arianna ignored the pushy detective and watched as two other male detectives whisked Cosmo away to the opposite side of the loft. "Wait! I need to see Cosmo! I need to ask him what happened," Arianna cried out, still standing up, ready to run towards Cosmo. Detective Baynor placed her hands-on Arianna's shoulders and forced her back down on the couch.

"I need to see him…" Arianna started. Just then, the medical examiner's office wheeled Kris' body past on a gurney. Kris was covered in a black body bag. All of the air in Arianna's lungs seemed to rush from her body in a whoosh. At first, she opened her mouth, and no sound came out. But then, she could hear her own voice at an ear-shattering pitch.

"Oh, my God!! Oh my God!!" Arianna cried out as she stared at the body bag. "What did I do?! What did I do?!" she moaned over and over. Detective Baynor shot a look at the uniformed officers standing around the loft. This was what she'd been waiting to hear. Any admission of guilt was what the detective needed to get Arianna in cuffs.

"Arianna, how did you get the blood all over your clothes?" Detective Baynor moved in for the kill while she had Arianna emotional. "You are asking yourself what did you do... we want to know what you did too. We want to help you sort this all out, Arianna," Detective Baynor pushed. Arianna turned towards the detective with her eyes squinted into dashes. What the fuck didn't she understand!

"I told you! I don't know! I can't remember!!" Arianna growled, losing her breath as she punched her fists into the leather arm of the couch. She drew blood on her knuckles. Detective Baynor noticed that both of Arianna's hands looked pretty rough like she'd been fighting.

Detective Baynor signaled another male detective to follow her to the other side of the room. "She appears to have defensive wounds on her hands and scratches on her face. I think a fight over Mr. Lover Boy over there got way out of hand. Add in the meth paraphernalia that we found, and boom, murder," Detective Baynor ran down her theory to her counterpart. They both watched Arianna as they whispered about her. She held her head in her hands and rocked feverishly. Looked like she was hiding something to them. Detective Baynor shrugged. She thought she definitely had her case in the bag.

"I think we need to take Ms. Arianna Epstein down to the squad and get to the bottom of her version about what really happened. Although I think I already have it all figured out," Detective Baynor said. She nodded her head at the three uniformed officers that were flanking the couch where Arianna sat. "Let's keep the media out of this for now," Detective Baynor whispered. With their murder suspect being the daughter of Levi Epstein and granddaughter of the late Ari Epstein and the dead girl being the daughter of Deana Shepherd, this case could turn into a media circus very quickly.

"Ms. Epstein, please stand up," one of the officers instructed. Arianna's eyes went wide, and her eyebrows furrowed with confusion.

"Am I under arrest? What is going on?" she asked, her heart galloping in her chest.

"We just want to ask you some questions down at the precinct," the officer said flatly.

"Ms. Epstein, you have the right to remain silent. If you chose to give up that right, anything you say can and will be used against you in a court of law…" a female uniformed officer droned as she prodded Arianna to stand up.

"Why? I didn't do anything! I mean…I…I…don't remember! I didn't kill anyone!" Arianna belted out. She felt hands on her arms. Arianna pushed the officer's hands away. "I can stand on my own," she cried. The officer snatched her hand away and waited for Arianna to fall in line.

Arianna stood up, and the female uniformed officer handcuffed her and began a pat-down search of Arianna's person. "I need to call my father!" Arianna cried out. "He will have all of your jobs! This is not right!" No one responded to her tirade. As she was being prepared to be escorted out of the loft, Arianna caught sight of Cosmo, who was being interviewed by two male detectives. "Cosmo! Help me out of this! Please tell them what happened!" Arianna begged over and over again as she was led out of the loft in handcuffs. "Cosmo…please! Tell them I didn't do it!" Arianna's pleas fell on deaf ears; Cosmo didn't even look in her direction.

Chapter Nine
Shelby's Drama

Shelby lay curled up in her old bedroom inside of her parent's Hamptons estate. She'd been there since the party spectacle, unable to stop reliving the worst moment of her life over and over again. Shelby's usually vibrant face was now drained of color. Her always perfectly coiffed hair, now a tangled bird's nest atop her head; her eyes red-rimmed from crying and she could surely use a shower. Shelby hadn't left her room, much less her parent's house since the whole scene with Levi and Evelyn had literally exploded in all their faces. Her mother had been very supportive, but Miles Frankel, her father hadn't said two words to her since the revelation of her affair with Levi. Shelby had been his little girl, innocent in all rights. She couldn't even imagine what her father must think of her now. The thought made Shelby cry even harder.

Diane and Shelby sat together and burned the pictures Evelyn had dropped on Diane that night. Shelby cried her eyes out over and over again at how stupid she'd been to think it was all going to work out with Levi. She had believed him when he said he would leave Evelyn and be with her. Shelby didn't even think about how terrible it would look. She was young, dumb, and in love for the first time. Shelby was the talk of the Hamptons now, and she knew it. It wouldn't be long before the news traveled to New York City once the summer ended and everyone closed up their Hamptons hideaways and went back to their high-priced high rises in Manhattan. The thought of what they must be saying about her caused Shelby to shudder. Homewrecker was one of the nicer monikers she had picked up since her affair had been revealed. She had received over sixty text messages and at least forty calls from friends and family members who'd either witnessed the fiasco or had heard about it through the Hampton's grapevine. Shelby had ignored every single call and text. Levi had called the most, leaving pleading messages and sending groveling text messages. He'd said he was sorry, but Shelby didn't believe him. She saw the look on his face when his wife called Shelby a whore, and Levi didn't look the least bit offended. Shelby was devastated that she had just been another one of Levi's conquests. Shelby had ignored all of Levi's calls and had erased his last few messages before fully listening to them. Shelby knew she'd been playing with fire messing with a married man that was so close to her own family, but the attraction she had to Levi had been so magnetic she'd lost sight of the consequences. It was all too much to deal with. She wanted to bury her head and never come back out, but something else had suddenly gotten her attention.

A knock on her bedroom door drew Shelby up off her bed. She padded over to the door, barely wanting to pick up her feet. Wrapped in a soft, pink chenille robe, Shelby swallowed hard and exhaled as she put her face close to the door.

"Who is it?" Shelby called out from behind the locked door. She was silently praying it wasn't her mother again. Diane had been driving Shelby crazy, trying to get Shelby to get out of bed and cheer up. There was no way Shelby could deal with her mother right now.

"It's me, Annie," a soft, melodic voice whispered in return. Shelby could tell from the muffled sound of the voice; Annie had her face up against the door. Shelby's shoulders slumped with relief. She was glad it wasn't her mother for a change. Diane had tried to get Shelby to leave the room, offering her a free day at the spa, to go car shopping, shoe shopping, which Diane knew as Shelby's favorite. Shelby had refused all of her mother's offers. She couldn't imagine going out in public right now. The thought made her cringe and feel nauseous.

Shelby twisted the doorknob and unlocked the door. Looking out of the door suspiciously, Shelby grabbed the arm of the short, portly, black woman standing there and snatched her through the door and closed it back. Shelby locked the door behind them. She was glad, yet nervous as hell to see Annie. "Thanks for doing this Annie," Shelby huffed, on the brink of tears again for the fifth time that day. Annie's eyes were wide with fear like she'd committed a crime. She swiped the sweat from her forehead and let out a long sigh of relief. Annie had prayed all the way to Shelby's room that she didn't run into Diane. There would've been way too many questions. One thing Annie was not—a good liar.

"Girl, Shel, I'm telling you, all these secrets, I just can't take it," Annie huffed, wiping at the invisible sweat again. "I'm a God-fearing woman. I hate all the lies and sneaking. And if you're mother found out... lawd," Annie followed up, fanning at her face for air. She had been a part of the Frankel family for twenty-two years. Annie had served as Shelby's nanny when she was a child. The Frankel's kept her on the payroll even after Shelby had grown up. Annie was like a part of their family, and she kept things in the house flowing smoothly. Since Shelby was grown now, Annie took on the task of making sure Diane's household chores never piled up, especially the cooking. As wealthy as Miles was, he never liked to eat out, he'd prefer Annie's home cooking over a fancy restaurant any day. Annie was just a part of their family now, period. She loved Shelby like Shelby was her own child and in turn, Shelby confided in Annie more than she did her own mother. Shelby had been scared to face Annie when the scandal broke, but Annie was the only person she could trust right then. Annie had told Shelby the truth about how she felt about her affair, but right after, Annie had hugged her tight and told her it would be all right.

"Did my mother see you leave to go out?" Shelby asked nervously. Her stomach did flip-flops.

"No Shel, I don't think that she did. She went out I believe...hair appointment or something like that. But you know she'll be back soon, and the first place she is coming is right to this room," Annie answered, her eyebrows furrowed with worry. She had been doing nothing but worrying since Shelby took to hiding out in her room. But now this...

"Ok, did you get it?" Shelby asked, biting down on her bottom lip. Shelby was moving like she had to urinate really badly.

"Yes, I did," Annie answered, digging into her pocketbook. "And I didn't like it one bit. Imagine me buying this stuff at my age...the stares I got in that store. This is just too much Shel. Too much," Annie complained as she pulled a small plastic bag from her pocketbook and extended it towards Shelby.

Shelby's hands trembled as she snatched the bag and looked at Annie through glassy eyes.

"Oh my God Annie, I could never repay you for this," Shelby said, her voice cracking. Annie twisted her lips and scrunched her eyebrows. It was an expression that was all too familiar to Shelby. She'd seen it over the years, anytime she did something Annie didn't agree with that was the face she got. Annie wasn't much on using admonishing words, but her body language most of the time said it all.

"Please. Not that face. Not now. Not you too," Shelby grumbled, wrapping her arms around herself. "I've been through enough. And now this…I don't need you of all people to judge me, Annie, please. Not right now of all the times in my life," Shelby said, tearing up. Annie softened her face and touched Shelby's hand gently. She hated to see Shelby cry. Annie still thought of Shelby as her little girl. She had basically raised Shelby.

"I'm not one to judge you, baby; you know that. God is the only one who can judge you. But this isn't right. It just isn't right. Nothing about none of it is right Shel," Annie said softly. "Nothing about this situation can sit right with any God you serve. I'm gonna be here for you no matter what, but I want you to think about this long and hard. That man is married Shel… he is married to your mother's friend," Annie scolded sounding more like a mother than a former nanny.

"It was a mistake. I know everyone hates me, but I'm not perfect. It was a big mistake," Shelby sobbed, lowering her eyes. She hated when Annie was disappointed in her. As a child, letting Annie down was the one thing that could be used to punish Shelby.

"Oh, Shel...I don't mean to be hard, but you know right from wrong. You are better than this. I taught you better than this. I hope you learned a valuable lesson with all of this mess. Now you need to get your own man and get married and have babies the right way. Do you hear me? You get your babies the right way," Annie said sternly. Shelby still looked down at the floor. Annie grabbed her into a tight embrace, her ample bosom providing a cushion. She squeezed Shelby close. "I will always love you no matter how many mistakes you make," Annie whispered in her ear. Shelby let out more loud sobs.

"I hope it comes back negative," Shelby whimpered into the material of Annie's shirt.

"For the good of everyone involved, I hope it does too," Annie said with feeling.

Chapter Ten
Kosta & Levi

*K*osta Stoychavic was an unassuming man, standing only five feet, ten inches tall with a protruding gut and flat feet. His appearance didn't matter; his power and reputation was what preceded him. Although unassuming to the eye, Kosta was the third man from the top in the hierarchy of the Brooklyn faction of the Russian mafia. Kosta sat flanked by four of his men, who were all dressed in black. It was like something out of a movie for sure. Kosta took a long pull from his Russian cigar and blew the smoke out slowly. He seemed to be pondering the information he'd just received. His intelligence was being insulted; he could tell that much. Finally, Kosta looked across the table at Levi and nodded his head. Kosta wanted to hear it again…in a different way. He wanted to make sure he heard it correctly before he reacted.

"So Epstein, tell me again, why I can't draw down the funds you tell me for years were in my account," Kosta asked, his accent thick. Kosta coolly took another long pull on his cigar. He held his breath extra-long, letting the effects of the smoke rush to his head.

Kosta had been putting millions of dollars into Levi Epstein's hands for the past six years, and according to the statements he received from Epstein Trading, Kosta was of the belief that he had earned over six million on his investments. Kosta had heard things about Levi's recent business dealings, and he wanted to collect his money. Both men had their eyes locked in on one another, except Kosta was cool, and Levi had his toes balled up inside his Ferragamos. Levi's stomach was also knotted like a nautical rope. The tension in the room was thick. Levi cleared his throat; the sound seemed more pronounced in the eerily silent space. He had thought about what he was going to say, and he just wasn't sure it was going to fly with Kosta.

"I told you, the SEC regulates all of the accounts. It is out of my hands until I meet all of their requirements. I just need time to get the funds wired back to you. I already have my assistant working on that," Levi fabricated on the spot. He was silently praying that his most notorious client bought the story. The truth was, Levi was silently wracking his brain to think of how he would get his hands on that kind of money at a time like this. He wiped at invisible sweat on his forehead. Kosta laughed heartily and then he looked at his men, and they started laughing as well. Kosta found it really funny that Levi thought he was so stupid. Levi's eyes grew wide. He flexed his neck and exhaled. It wasn't going to be so easy to convince Kosta, Levi reasoned with himself. "I am trying my best Kosta...there are rules..." Levi stammered.

"Epstein, do you think I am dumb because I came to this country from the Czech Republic as a poor man starving for a chance?" Kosta asked calmly; his face was devoid of any emotion. He stared at Levi and leaned into the table that separated them. Levi's lip quivered under Kosta's glare.

"Kosta, I've been dealing with you for years. You know

that I wouldn't ever think you were dumb. I have nothing but respect for you," Levi replied, putting his hands up in a halting motion. "I will have your money. I have to follow procedures... you know. Just give me a few days," Levi continued nervously. He swallowed the ball of nerves sitting at the back of his throat. If he could get up and run, he would. Levi looked around at the other men who were all staring down at him. He knew running was not an option.

Kosta lifted his left hand in the air, signaling over one of the four men that flanked him. A tall, blonde, with icy blue eyes, a barrel chest and square shoulders stepped behind Levi. Levi whirled his head around frantically. His heart jumped in his chest. The man was perilously close to him. Levi could feel his breath on him. Kosta made a hand motion. The blonde man bore down on Levi like an attack animal given the order.

"Kosta...listen. I...I'm going to..." Levi stuttered, his eyes wide as dinner plates. The blonde man grabbed Levi's right hand and held it flat against the table. Levi squirmed in his chair. He could only imagine what was to come. "Kosta! Please! Don't do this! Please!" Levi begged, his voice rising three octaves. He struggled against the blonde man's grip but was no match for the hulk of a man. Kosta stood up; amused at the sight of this little weasel Jew thief.

"I don't like to be jerked around. You may play games with your other clients, but not with me. The one thing I don't play around with is my money, and my intelligence...you have insulted me," Kosta said calmly, an eerily sinister grin painting his face. He reached down and grinded the fire lit end of his cigar into the flesh of Levi's hand. For a moment, time seemed to stand still in the room.

"Aggh!" Levi screamed, jerking his body in the chair. The pain climbed from his hand all the way up to his arm. Spit flew out of Levi's mouth, and his chin fell into his chest. "Gaaa!" he wailed as he rocked back and forth. The man continued to hold Levi there. Satisfied that Levi was in excruciating pain, Kosta got close to Levi's face.

"This is just the beginning of what will happen to you if you don't arrange my money to go to my offshore account by the end of the week. Your face will be next. Then your daughter and wife and maybe that little blonde beauty you cheat on your wife with…you know the one you call your assistant," Kosta whispered harshly, his stale cigar breath shooting up Levi's nostrils. The blonde man loosened his grip on Levi. Levi was having a hard time catching his breath.

Levi used his right hand to hold his throbbing, painful left hand. "Ahh!" He rocked back and forth as the pain of the burn continued to radiate up his arm. "God help me," Levi murmured as Kosta, and his men exited his office. "God, help me." He didn't know what he would do now. Things had finally gotten to be too much to handle.

"Who is that coming out of Epstein's office?" Agent Assisi asked elbowing Agent Kemp on his arm to wake him up. Agent Kemp jumped and instinctively raised his professional-grade binoculars and adjusted them. He squinted through the large round lenses and frowned.

"Shit!" he exclaimed. "Hand me the long lens quick!" Kemp urged, his hand flapping in anticipation. Assisi scrambled to reach into the back seat for the camera. He hastily threw it to Kemp. Kemp held it up to his eye and began clicking rapidly.

They couldn't afford to miss this moment.

"What is it? Who is that?" Assisi asked impatiently as Kemp continued to click the camera lens.

"Looks like Epstein stepped in shit with the Russian mafia. That's Kosta Stoychavic! The number three in the Russian mafia. Dangerous. Fuck!" Kemp cursed, punching the car door.

"What? What does this mean?" Assisi asked, staring at the men through the windshield. He was confused. Russian mafia? Epstein? What?

"It means to save our case and our subject; we may have to go over on this case quicker than we thought. Epstein probably took money from them, and if he can't produce returns, he'll end up in the Hudson River before we could ever snag his ass. That blood will be on our hands too. Call Vargas right away," Kemp rambled off, as he continued to snap pictures.

Chapter Eleven
Evelyn's Call

Evelyn jumped out of her sleep to her cell phone ringing on the hotel's nightstand. It was strange since Levi nor Arianna ever called her anymore. Not even to say hello. Evelyn unhooked her body from Max's clutch, and blindly grabbed for her phone. Barely able to get her eyes to focus, Evelyn squinted at the small screen. Finally, she was able to see that it read UNKNOWN. Evelyn sighed and closed her eyes again. Evelyn started to press ignore, but a feeling in the pit of her stomach told her to pick up. Whoever was calling her, it must've been important. Leaning away from Max, Evelyn held the phone tightly to her ear, just in case, it was Levi. She needed to make sure the call would be obscured from Max's earshot.

"Hello?" Evelyn breathed into the receiver, her head flat on the pillow. Immediately goosebumps covered Evelyn's body in response to the sound filtering through the receiver. "Hello? Ari?" Evelyn's voice went high, and her eyes widened. She shoved Max's arm completely off of her and shot up in the bed. "Ari?! Arianna what is it?! Please Ari...calm down. I can't understand what you're saying!" Evelyn exclaimed frantically. Her heart immediately started hitting up against her breastbone with the force of a jackhammer on concrete. Evelyn was on her feet in one swift motion. She was no longer worried about Max overhearing her conversation. Max shot up in the bed, alarmed at the high-pitched tone of Evelyn's voice. His eyes were round like marbles; his mouth slack with confusion. "Evelyn, what is it?" Max asked, groggily, scrubbing his hand over his face in an effort to wipe away the sleep cobwebs. Evelyn halted him with her hand and gave him her back. Now wasn't the time to be responsive to Max. She needed a minute of privacy to speak to her daughter. Max was going to have to understand that. Only God knew what it could be given Arianna's history, and Evelyn wasn't about to risk it. Max craned his neck and furrowed his brow at her brisk reaction. He was taken aback. He sat back on the bed and watched her speak to her daughter in a panicked tone. Max listened intently. Everything Evelyn did was of interest to him. These were the times he had to put on his Special Agent Vargas hat and leave model boy Max to the side. Anything suspicious, the real Agent Vargas was fully interested and tuned in. He sat on the edge of the bed listening intently.

"Who! What! Where! When did this happen?! How Ari! Oh, my God! Ok, sweetheart, calm down. I'm on my way!" Evelyn exclaimed, her words coming out rapid-fire. She had a look of horror painting her face. "I'm coming!" Evelyn threw her phone down on the bed and raced around in circles. She mumbled under her breath and flailed her arms like she didn't know where to begin—get dressed; call Levi or run out of the hotel room. Max watched her for a few minutes, and then he decided to act. He slid off of the bed, swiped his long hair back and walked over to where Evelyn was standing going in circles. Max grabbed her around the waist. He wanted to stop her for a minute…help her gather her thoughts. "No! I have to go! I have to go!" Evelyn shouted, pushing at his strong arms. Max held her tighter. "Not now! My daughter needs me! I have to get out of here! I should've been home for her!" Evelyn screamed angrily. She was already blaming herself. Max just tightened his grip and pulled her close to his chest. He knew Evelyn was in no shape to leave like that.

"Shhh. Wait. Evelyn…sweetheart, take a minute to calm down," Max soothed, holding her tightly like she was a mental patient in need of a straitjacket. "Tell me what is going on. Please, Evelyn, please a' talk to me." Evelyn finally relented. Max wasn't giving up, and she didn't really want him to. Her body seemed to go limp against his. The rise and fall of his chest and steady thud of his heart comforted her. Max eased his grip a little and moved her away so he could look down into her face. Evelyn's face displayed horror. For the first time, Evelyn looked old to Max. It was as if worry lines and crow's feet suddenly cropped up on her face after the call.

"Talk to me," he said softly, looking in her glassy eyes. "I want to help. I want to be here for you Evelyn…that's all." Max's facial expression was sympathetic yet serious. Evelyn closed her eyes for a minute and put her face in her hands. She didn't know if sharing this with Max was the right thing, but she also felt alone.

"It's my daughter," Evelyn whispered, her mouth feeling like she'd eaten an entire jar of children's glue paste. "That was her on the phone. She's been arrested," Evelyn continued, shaking her head like a lost child. Max's facial expression changed. It was a mixture of sympathy and shock. He could only imagine what was going on. Evelyn had told him a little bit about her daughter; none of it particularly positive.

"I'm so sorry. What a' happened? Did she do something serious? Did something happen to her?" he asked, his mind racing a mile a minute. He tried to think of all of the things agents Kemp and Assisi would ask him. This was definitely something that had to be reported. Vargas wasn't too happy to have to deal with the local police either.

"I really don't know what happened Max. It's all so much. She couldn't talk long...she was so upset. Screaming and crying. Something about a girl named Kris being dead, and the police blaming Arianna for the death," Evelyn relayed ruefully. Max didn't speak. He was a bit dumbfounded. "Max, I don't know. But I have to go. I know my family may not be the greatest, but they're all I have. Really, I have to go. I'm sorry for pulling you into my mess of a life. I'm really sorry that you have to deal with all of this...first the party fiasco...now this," Evelyn told him solemnly. Max released her and put his hands up in surrender. He had heard enough. He was itching to call his FBI counterparts to get them on the case of finding out what the hell was really going on.

"Ok. I understand. I will wait for your call me," he told her. "You know if you need me, you can a' just call me."

Evelyn gave him a halfhearted smile. She finally began getting dressed. She looked around the hotel room, and her legs suddenly got weak. She flopped down on the bed and began sobbing loudly. The false sense of calm that Max had given her a few minutes prior didn't last long. Max sat next to her and went to put his arm around her quaking shoulders. The weight of it all had finally settled on her like a five-hundred-ton anvil.

"Please...don't," Evelyn cried, waving him away. For

the first time, an overwhelming feeling of shame about her affair with Max seemed to have a stronghold on her conscience. Maybe if I wasn't here with him, I would've been there for Arianna. She's in this mess because of me. Evelyn had a migraine after thinking about it all.

"Max...really. I've done enough damage with this... with us," Evelyn sobbed, her honesty sending bat-sized butterflies into her stomach. "I don't know what I was thinking. I've been so busy being shameless, just like Levi, that I lost sight of everything that should have been important to me. I let my daughter suffer because I was so hell-bent on revenge again her father. Now, look at what I've done. My daughter is in terrible trouble, and it's all my damn fault."

Max stood up and walked away from Evelyn. He turned his back and sighed loudly. Max knew what was coming next. "So, what does this all mean Evelyn...I mean for us. For me?"

"I'm sorry Max, but I can't see you anymore," Evelyn said flatly, trying to get her emotions together. She had to be there for Arianna, even if it meant letting Max and her deep feelings for him go.

"You don't mean that... I know you're upset," Max replied.

"I mean it! If I wasn't here being an adulterous whore my daughter wouldn't be in this mess!" Evelyn snapped. She meant it.

"Just go to your daughter. If you need me, I am always here," Max told her. He watched as Evelyn stormed out of the hotel room, this time she didn't leave a gift or any cash.

Max rushed over to his pants and picked up his cell phone. He noticed that he had six missed calls. He recalled the last number and pressed the connect button.

"Vargas!" the voice on the other rushed in as he picked up.

"Yeah."

"Don't let Evelyn Epstein out of your fucking sight. We just found out that her husband is in deep with the Russian mafia. They may go after her, and we need her to stay safe, or all of this would have been for nothing," Kemp belted into the phone.

"Too late. She just left," Vargas said.

"Well, you better find her. Find her fast!" Kemp screamed frantically.

Marcellos Vargas hung up the phone and tossed it across the room. "Fuck!" he cursed, flexing his jaw. He grabbed his undercover garb and slid into the jeans and tight fitted top. He had his work cut out for him.

"She said her daughter was arrested…a fucking million precincts in New York!" Vargas grumbled as he headed out the door. He had to find Evelyn and tell her everything before something terrible happened.

Chapter Twelve
More than Arianna Can Handle

*A*rianna lifted her head when she heard the locks on the slate gray, metal door click. She rubbed her red-rimmed eyes as they adjusted to the light. She let out a long, exasperated breath when she saw who had entered the room. Not this bitch again. Arianna said to herself. She had definitely had enough.

Detective Baynor slammed a stack of files and a videotape down on the opposite side of the small, wobbly, metal table. Detective Baynor's face was stoic and hard-lined. She wore twenty-two years of police work like a mask, each worry line that cropped up near her mouth and wrinkled branching out from the corner of her eyes telling a different story of sleepless nights, dead people, and remorseless suspects. Detective Baynor had broken through the NYPD's glass ceiling, and she prided herself on her nearly perfect track record. She was known around the department for "always getting her man." No kids, no family, and no life outside of work made it easy for Detective Baynor to be the best of the best. She had dedicated her entire adult life to the police department, sometimes to a fault. Since becoming a detective, Baynor had not left any case unsolved and had elicited confessions in all but one of her cases. She was not about to let some rich, shameless, drug-addicted, murderous brat change that. She looked at Arianna with pure disgust. She was an example of everything Baynor hated in her life. Here was this little girl who'd been born with a silver spoon in her mouth, throwing her life away on drugs and murder. Baynor had already surmised that Arianna had never worked for anything a day in her life; the complete opposite of Baynor's own upbringing. Baynor had been born in Hell's Kitchen, had been abandoned by two drug-addicted parents who had never looked back. Baynor had knocked around in the old, archaic foster care system before anyone cared about finding foster children a loving, stable, home. Baynor had suffered abuse at the hands of several foster parents and always had to work extra hard just to make something of herself. She flexed her jaw, just thinking about it all. How senseless it was for these rich people to throw their lives away when they had the road paved for them. She had a low tolerance for the insolence of the rich.

"You ready to talk?" Detective Baynor asked, placing her hand on top of the videotape. It was a scare tactic that Baynor had been best at using within her unit. It almost always got a suspect talking. Arianna looked down at the tape and back at Baynor. "Well?" Baynor shifted her head to the side, drumming her fingers on the top of the tape. Her prop seemed to draw Arianna's attention like intended. Baynor felt a pang of excitement flit through her stomach. Conquering this little rich girl would do so much for Baynor. She could taste the vindication on her tongue.

Arianna looked down at the table, at the videotape and then placed her head back down on her folded arms. She wasn't going to say it again…she did not remember shit about the murder. All she knew was that she didn't do it. Detective Baynor could feel the heat rising from her feet, making its way up her body. She clenched her fists together. This little girl was really starting to push her buttons. The videotape prop had worked on grown, well-seasoned criminals. How dare this little girl make Baynor feel stupid! She moved to the edge of her seat, the large vein in her neck pulsing fiercely against her skin.

"Look, Ms. Epstein, I am only trying to help you help yourself. What we already know is that a girl is dead and that you were the last person seen with her. You had her blood all over you. Now I'm trying to find out why it happened. Maybe it was self-defense. Maybe she attacked you, and you took a weapon from her, and things just…just happened. Maybe everything that happened is all on this videotape, and I am trying to clarify why it happened," Detective Baynor opined, raising her eyebrows at Arianna. Arianna didn't budge. She kept her head down on the table, ignoring everything the detective was saying. Baynor closed her eyes for a quick second to compose herself. You get more bees with honey than with shit. You get more bees with honey…. Baynor chanted inside her head. She had to try and keep herself calm now.

"Ahem," she cleared her throat. "Arianna…you know this could be easier than you think. I'm trying to help you. I really am trying to be a sense of support for you. Here's what I can tell you…that building and your boyfriend's apartment had plenty of cameras around. We have access to all of that when something like this happens, you know, we can review those tapes," Baynor tried, tapping her pen on the videotape. Arianna lifted her head and stared at Detective Baynor with a glazed over look in her eyes.

"If you have the murder on that tape, then I need to see it because I already told you I don't know what happened. Maybe I can learn something new from you too…since you already think you know what happened. You don't really need my help detective," Arianna deadpanned. She wasn't trying to be difficult, but this detective acted as if she didn't understand English. The line had been drawn in the sand. The tension in the room was so thick it was almost palpable.

Detective Baynor leaned into the table, her face drawn into a tight scowl. "Now you fucking listen here you little trust fund bitch!" Detective Baynor started, but the sound of the door locks clicking interrupted her tirade. Both Baynor and Arianna jumped at the sound of the steel door clanging open. Baynor whirled her neck around so hard she almost gave herself whiplash. Arianna popped up as well. Neither of them knew what to expect.

"That'll be enough, detective. My client does not wish to speak on this matter until she has had time to consult with me," a male voice droned. Arianna and Detective Baynor looked up at the tall, slender, black man standing in the doorway flanked by two uniformed officers. He displayed a smile revealing a perfect set of gleaming, white teeth.

"Aaron Collins, Ms. Epstein's attorney. I can't say it's nice to meet you, detective, maybe if these were better circumstances," the man said smiling wide and holding his card out in front of him between his pointer and middle fingers.

Detective's Baynor's jaw rocked feverishly as she grabbed the man's card; threw it on top of her pile of fake evidence and grabbed it all up into her arms. Her heart pounded in her chest, and she could feel the adrenaline rushing through her veins. She wanted to punch a wall or kick something, the urges almost overwhelming her. Before Baynor left the room, the detective turned towards Arianna with fire flashing in her eyes. Her nostrils flared, and audible breaths of air escaped them. She stepped in front of Arianna's attorney so that Arianna had no choice but to look at her.

"Having money can only get you so far. The truth and its karmic consequences always prevail. You may have had everything laid out for you in life…but one thing is for sure little miss sunshine…you will not get away with murder on my watch," Detective Baynor gritted, locking eyes with Arianna. Arianna rolled her eyes and looked to her attorney for help.

"That's enough contact with my client detective. I think you are one step from being out of line. I know plenty of folks downtown at IAB, so you had better quit while you are ahead and leave us alone," Collins said as he slid into the chair across from Arianna. Detective Baynor backed down. She held up her left hand, signaling her retreat, but her face said something totally different. It wasn't over. That was for sure. Baynor was not going to quit until she had this case all ready for the prosecutors. She would not rest until Arianna was indicted for the murder.

Arianna's shoulders slumped. She hung her head and exhaled. She had never felt so relieved in her entire life. Maybe her mother wasn't as fucked up as she'd grown up to believe. At least her mother answered her phone and got her an attorney… not like her father, who Arianna had called first and still hadn't heard a word from.

Cosmo's hand shook as he lit the cigarette one of the male detectives had given him. Cosmo took a long drag on the cigarette and blew the smoke out in a long huff. He had had enough run-ins with the law to know that the goodwill gesture of the cigarette was part of their buttering up. Cosmo had seen it in movies too…police giving suspects things like cigarettes, coffee, and food to get the suspect comfortable enough to talk. Cosmo was smarter than that. He took the cigarette, but they couldn't trick him. He had told them his story and he was sticking to it. Cosmo thought he was way too smart to get caught up in his own story. Playing it cool was his plan. He blew out another long stream of smoke

"So, let's get this straight. The girl we're holding down here, Arianna Epstein, told you the night before the murder, that if she couldn't have you, no one else was going to have you? You? Really? You?" Detective Ron Ledbetter repeated, his fingers steepled in front of him. If he had it his way, Detective Ledbetter would've had a little roughing up session with Cosmo before talking to him, but he knew the case was going to get lots of media attention real soon. Ledbetter didn't like anything about Cosmo. He knew the little, slim ball was a weasel that preyed on rich girls. He also didn't believe a thing that came out of Cosmo's little, thin, lying lips.

Cosmo blew more smoke from between his lips. "Look, man. I told you this story ten different ways," Cosmo said, sitting up straight in the hard-wooden chair. He thought if he looked straight at the detective that would somehow make him more credible. "It's like I said before, Ari came home from rehab, but she still wanted to get stoned. Once a junkie, always a junkie. Do you know what I mean? I was her supplier when I used to deal. I don't sell drugs anymore you know," Cosmo relayed, looking directly at the detective to see if his story was making a dent in the doubt clouding the detective's face. Ledbetter let out a long sigh, then a grunt.

"I mean we messed around here and there, but she's jail bait in my eyes. She came to club Torrid the other night searching for me...you can ask the bouncers they'll tell you. I didn't even want to be bothered, but she begged them to let her in to see me. She stormed in on Kris, and I. Ari started cursing at Kris telling her she wanted to be with me and that if she couldn't have me, no one would. Kris got in her face, but being that I am the man that I am, I came between them. No sense in letting two girls fight over little ole' me," Cosmo said, smiling like the story was amusing. It was starting to sound good. Half of it was true, so he just knew he had it in the bag.

Detective Ledbetter exhaled a windstorm of breath. He knew Cosmo was full of shit, but he wanted to get him on the record. "So, then what?" Ledbetter asked, tapping his foot under the table impatiently. "She went from proclaiming her undying love for you to killing a girl? So, was it because you are the best dick on this side of the East coast? I mean, what is it? You're so good you got girls willing to kill over you?" Ledbetter summed up, his lips twisted in disbelief. Cosmo rolled his eyes at the detective's snide remarks.

"Then, I told Arianna to get lost. She offered me ten thousand dollars to be her friend again. She was known for that...buying friends. Just ask any of the rock stars' daughters they all know the real Arianna. She came by my condo with the cash, and when she saw Kris inside, she started going crazy. I calmed her down again and told her that Kris was my girl, and if she didn't like it, she could take her money and go. Arianna calmed down. She came inside, and Kris allowed her to hang out with us. They both wanted to get high. I tried to convince Arianna that she shouldn't do it. I mean…she had just gotten home from rehab. Must've been the biggest waste of time and money ever. Anyway, Arianna had some crank from her new dealer, since I got out of the business. She threw the money and the crank up on the table. All of a sudden she and Kris were best friends over that crank. They started jerking around together like best friends. Me…I don't dabble in that shit. I was watching them for a while, but I got bored with that real quick. Then, I got a call from my boy John. John needed me to come and help him take care of a problem, so I left the condo to go see about the problem with him. When I returned, I found all of you dudes crawling all over my place and you know…Kris…Kris was dead," Cosmo finished, hanging his head for a good show of grief. "That's all I know," he finished up with a shrug.

Detective Ledbetter tilted his head and glared at Cosmo. *This kid has gotta be fucking shitting me if he thinks I believe that bullshit story he just told me.* Ledbetter thought. He put his elbows on the table and leaned in. "Something about your story stinks to holy hell kid. See, what I think is that you know a lot more than what you're letting on. I also believe you're a fucking liar from the bottom of your feet to the top of your head. One thing I know for sure is the truth will come out," Ledbetter said seriously. He wanted Cosmo to know he wasn't a rookie. This wasn't his first go around the block on a homicide. Cosmo stayed calm, though. He stubbed out his cigarette on the table and disrespectfully flicked the butt into the corner of the room.

"Just tell me if I am a witness or suspect, so I know

whether to call my lawyer or not," Cosmo replied snidely. He was sick of this abuse. But Ledbetter was equally tired of Cosmo.

Detective Ledbetter jumped to his feet and grabbed Cosmo's collar from across the table. Ledbetter yanked Cosmo up out of the chair and pulled him halfway onto the table so he could meet him face to face. "You little piece of shit. I know you were getting those girls high…it was your drugs and I want to know what you did that killed that little girl. I'm not going to let you send another innocent girl up the river because you're a fucking slimeball," Ledbetter gritted. The door flung open, and the two detectives that had been recording the meeting behind the double-sided glass rushed into the room. "C'mon Leddy… let him go. It's not worth it," they urged, pulling Ledbetter by the waist. "Just let him go man…he's not worth it," they prodded some more.

"Let me tell you something you little drug dealing, mafia wanna-be. I will find out what role you played in that girl's death, and I will make sure you hang from your balls in the town square for everyone to see. I see your type all of the time, and you think you're so fucking untouchable…well you got a fucking surprise coming your way by way of me," Ledbetter gritted, his breath hot on Cosmo's face. Something inside of Ledbetter wouldn't allow him to let Cosmo go. He was seeing his own struggles with his drug-addicted daughter come to the forefront of his brain. It was a painful topic for Ledbetter and everyone knew it.

"Ron, man… let him go. C'mon he isn't worth it," Detective Sharky said, still pulling Ledbetter from behind. "He's a two-time punk. Don't get into a mess with IAB over this loser," Sharky urged some more. Cosmo was starting to turn as red as a freshly cooked lobster. That was all the detectives needed right now…a police brutality charge.

Detective Ledbetter loosened his grip on Cosmo and sent his face slamming into the table. "Ahh! Fuck! You fucker!" Cosmo screamed out as his nose busted open and began spilling blood like a knocked over fire hydrant. "I'll have your fucking head for this!" Cosmo screeched, trying to use his hand to quell the bleeding.

"Get him out of here!" Sharky yelled to his counterparts. They grabbed Detective Ledbetter and dragged him out. Just as they were leaving, Detective Baynor approached. She stood in the doorway and watched as Cosmo tried to stop the bleeding from his nose with the sleeve of his jacket.

"What's going on here?" Detective Baynor asked, looking at the overturned chair and bleeding witness.

"Things got a little heated," Detective Sharky answered as he started out the door. There wasn't much else to say.

"Let me get a few minutes alone with him," Detective Baynor said. Sharky looked at her with a raised eyebrow.

"Aren't you supposed to be working on the girl?" he asked.

"She lawyered up. I think that's confession enough for me. Especially if I can get this one to officially sign on as a witness," Baynor answered. Detective Sharky smirked. Hadn't Baynor done her homework? Cosmo was a well-known drug dealer.

"This guy is as credible as Hannibal Lector. Put him on the stand and no jury worth their salt will believe him unless he says he was standing there when the murder happened," Sharky replied.

"Well, whatever it takes. I need to get this case solved. I'm not going to let my perfect record be tarnished by the fucking rich and shameless. Not that little spoiled brat down there of all people," Detective Baynor retorted. Sharky shrugged and moved out of her way. Baynor stepped into the room and closed the door behind her.

"Constantine Sipriano...or Cosmo as your friends call you. I'm detective Baynor. I hear you're going to be my star witness against Arianna Epstein," Detective Baynor said, extending a wad of tissues towards Cosmo as a peace offering. Cosmo snatched the tissue and started cleaning up his face. "Where do you want me to start? Oh...I got a lot to say about little miss rich girl," Cosmo said, his voice nasally. Baynor smiled. Those were the words she'd been dying to hear. She liked Cosmo and what he had to say already.

Chapter Thirteen
The 1st Precinct

*E*velyn was clearly out of her element. Dressed in premium designer clothes and shockingly sparkly jewels, Evelyn stuck out like a sore thumb in the precinct. She clutched a wad of damp tissues as she sat on a hard, wooden wall bench inside the lobby of the 1st precinct. Evelyn was too lost in her own problems to even notice some of the rough characters floating around her. She'd watched as uniformed police officers had dragged their evening collars in. Some of the handcuffed perpetrators looked rough, and others looked like everyday people. Every few seconds, Evelyn dabbed at the tears that threatened to escape her eyes. She had been an emotional mess since Arianna's call. It was a wonder Evelyn had even made it to the precinct. She had felt so lost when her daughter called and told her that she'd been arrested. After the initial shock, Evelyn had at least had the wherewithal to call their family attorney, Aaron Collins, to meet there after the nerve-wracking call she had received from Arianna. "Murder? Am I hearing you correctly, Mrs. Epstein?" Collins had repeated during their phone conversation. Usually, when he got calls from the Epsteins, it would be regarding Levi's business dealings or DUIs that Levi had amassed, nothing as serious as this. Collins had sounded a bit caught off guard, but he quickly changed his mindset when Evelyn told him she needed him right away.

Once Evelyn had heard the word murder reiterated, Evelyn thought it sounded strange and eerie as well. How could her daughter be charged with murder? Arianna had been many things over the years, spoiled, pretentious, addicted, and out of control, but Evelyn knew her daughter wouldn't harm a fly. There was no way Evelyn would believe that Arianna had murdered anyone. Evelyn wasted no time after Collins had agreed to sign on to the case. She'd had her driver pick Collins up and accompany her to the precinct. The attorney had taken over once they'd confirmed Arianna had been brought in for questioning and was in an interrogation room down in the belly of the dank, old, building that housed the precinct. Evelyn had chosen to wait rather than accompanying Collins to see about Arianna. Evelyn didn't think she could take much more emotional battering. She didn't know how her daughter would react to having her there, and she was too mentally fragile to find out. It could be hit or miss with Arianna. There had been many times Arianna had called Evelyn for help but treated Evelyn horribly after the help was rendered.

Evelyn dug into her Birkin bag and picked up her cell phone. With trembling hands, she looked at the screen again. It had become like an every ten- second habit now. She was anxiously awaiting a call back from Levi. Where the hell is he? I can't believe he has not returned any of my calls. Obviously, he knows it is an emergency! Her mind raced with thoughts. She let out a long breath. There were at least six missed called from Max...nothing from Levi. Evelyn felt sick inside just thinking about what she'd done to Max. What she'd done to herself as well by cutting her relationship with Max. Max had been her outlet, her escape, and more importantly, he'd helped her get revenge on Levi. It was a game Evelyn had become used to playing. It occupied her time and her mind. She didn't know how she would survive her marriage…being a mother or life in general right now without the occasional getaway with Max. Evelyn shook off the thoughts. It is my duty to be here for my child. It is my duty to be here for my child. Evelyn chanted in her head as she dialed Levi's number for the tenth time. She got the same result as the nine previous calls. No answer. She left yet another message, this time, telling Levi where she was and what was going on. "Maybe that will draw him from between her legs," Evelyn mumbled out loud to herself. She could just picture Levi pressing the ignore button on his cell phone while Shelby lay sprawled on top of him. The two of them laughing each time Evelyn called like she was a big joke. Evelyn cringed at the visual playing in her head. She was completely lost in her own world of thoughts. But more disturbing, she was oblivious to her bustling and noisy surroundings.

"What happened? Can't find your man? Calling him… no answer, eh?" a voice boomed from Evelyn's left side. Evelyn jumped at the voice and the statement too. She was so lost in thought she had not seen the stranger that had come and sat a few inches away from her on the bench. Evelyn furrowed her brow and looked at the ugly faced, hulk of a man like he was a piece of garbage. He was minding her business. She didn't like it one bit. The man could read the expression on her face and immediately tried to soften his hard-lined permanent frown.

"I'm sorry…I don't mean to pry. You just look so

distressed. I see a beautiful one like you looking at her phone all along...must be looking for your man," the man continued, an ugly grin splayed across his face. Is he crazy! Evelyn's eyes hooded over. How dare this nobody interfere in her life at a time like this! She swallowed hard. Evelyn prided herself on always trying to keep her high-class, socially acceptable composure in public, but today was not the day to have this total stranger questioning her. Evelyn's mood was already on a hairpin trigger.

"Thanks. But I don't need questions or comfort from a stranger. Now if you will excuse me...please leave me alone," Evelyn snapped. This man had clearly reached over that imaginary societal boundary line. The man laughed. It was a hearty, maniacal laugh. His reaction shocked and scared Evelyn at the same time. The sound of his guttural gurgle of a laugh sent chills through Evelyn's body.

"So, I ask you again, are you missing your man? Are you in trouble...what is it? Why is a well-off person like you at a dirty place like this? I'm just trying to find out," the man continued with his prying questions only now he had slid closer to Evelyn. This was too much for her. New York City was filled with crazy people, but Evelyn hadn't had to deal with them much. Not with her usually sheltered existence in the big city. She was driven almost everywhere, and if she wasn't, she was always with family or friends. Taken aback, by the stranger's brash move, Evelyn prepared to stand up. Evelyn set her feet and gathered her pocketbook, and just as she went to stand up, the stranger grabbed her arm roughly. He dug his large, animal-like hand into the muscle of her forearm and pulled her back down. "Ouch!" she screamed, attempting to yank her arm away from this crazed lunatic. "Don't touch me!" Evelyn belted out hoping to get the attention of a police officer, but they were all moving so fast with their prisoners or preparing to end or begin their shift, no one really paid Evelyn any attention. The stranger pulled her closer to him. Evelyn choked out a short grunt, a weak attempt at a scream. She was forced so close to the stranger; that his face was up against her neck. "Please," Evelyn whimpered, the pain of his brutish hand radiating up her arm.

"Shhhh. Calm down. Don't make a scene, Mrs. Epstein. You should act like we are long lost friends…we kind of sorta' are long lost friends," the stranger whispered now. His breath hot on Evelyn's neck and ear. Evelyn's pulse quickened, and she immediately felt stomach sick. She had no idea how this disgusting man knew her name or even where to find her. "Please, I don't know what you want. If its money…" Evelyn started, she found herself involuntarily whispering now too. She was too afraid to scream for help for fear that the man would snap her arm right out of the socket. The man squeezed her arm even harder now. Unbearable pain shot up to her shoulder and radiated through her body. "Please…" she whimpered again, trying to make eye contact with any of the police officers who buzzed by like she didn't even exist. Evelyn was paralyzed with fear now, her entire body rigid. Tears were burning at the backs of her eye sockets like acid.

"Shhh. Don't talk. Keep your pretty little mouth shut and let me do the talking. I want you to tell your husband, Levi…the crook, that Kosta sent me to see you. Your husband will know who Kosta is for sure. He can explain to you why I am here like this. Tell Levi, Kosta sends a message for him again. Kosta knows you and your little girl, what you look like, where you live, where you shop, where you go to fuck your boyfriend and Kosta will come to see you again if Levi doesn't make good on the deals. Understand? Next time, I will do more than just grab your arm...yes, yes...much, much worse, trust me," the man hissed, with a nasty little chortle at the end of his threat. This time Evelyn realized the man had some kind of an accent. She was too frightened to immediately place it, but the man had a heavy accent nonetheless. Evelyn knew Levi had gotten himself into some deep troubles, but she could've never imagined anything like this. Threats to her and Arianna was a major deal in Evelyn's book. Levi had done things before, years of neglect and the like, but this...this was more than Evelyn could stand. She was powerless, and she realized that quickly.

"Please...my daughter and I have nothing to do with..." Evelyn began, her words rising and falling. The man didn't stay to listen. He quickly loosened his grip on Evelyn with a shove. And in what seemed like a flash of light, he got up and disappeared. It was the craziest thing she had ever experienced. Evelyn swung her head around frantically, but just as fast as the menacing stranger had appeared, he was gone. Evelyn placed her hand over her chest and inhaled. She was trying to get her heart rate to slow, but nothing worked. Her heart pounded so hard Evelyn thought it would jump loose from her chest. Evelyn's head swirled now with the worst migraine she'd ever experienced.

Evelyn didn't know what she had done to deserve all of the things happening to her and her family. She'd tried to live her life right. Giving to charities, going to church whenever she was in the country and even sometimes giving to the homeless people she saw on the streets of New York whenever she was out. I am definitely being punished for something. Evelyn had reasoned.

She dabbed at the new line of sweat that had materialized on her forehead. Again, she attempted to get to her feet. As she braced herself, she slumped back down for a quick second. Her legs felt weak like she'd just run ten miles. It was her nerves. "What is happening?" she whispered to herself. "What is happening to us," she cried into her wad of tissue. Just then a gaggle of commotion moved in Evelyn's direction. Evelyn widened her eyes. She couldn't take much more. The rumble of feet and voices gave her pause. Panic-stricken, Evelyn looked up, frantically trying to make sure she wasn't about to be accosted again. She noticed Aaron Collins, their attorney, amongst the noisy ball of bodies moving in her direction. Evelyn shot up onto her feet now. This time she was able to stand. She needed to know that Arianna was safe. That no one had gotten to her. Evelyn seemed to have a newfound strength in her entire body. A motherly boost of power propelled her up and towards her attorney. Evelyn's encounter with the stranger, now secondary in her mind, she rushed right into Collins. Her face streaked with worry.

"Collins…what is it? Is she alright? Did she eat? Has she been treated fairly?" Evelyn fired off questions in rapid succession. Collins put his hand up in a halting motion. His paper bag brown skin seemingly stretched tight with worry lines. Evelyn didn't like the way he looked. She'd never seen him look nothing other than cool under pressure. This time was different; his eyes seemed to say it all. That look didn't bode well with Evelyn. "What…tell me…" she demanded. It was all she could do to keep herself from slapping him and screaming TELL ME MY DAUGHTER WILL BE ALRIGHT! Collins pulled her by her elbow, urging her away from the crowd of detectives and police officers. Evelyn took his cue and moved close to him. Her insides were churning with nerves.

"Look, Evelyn, Arianna is ok. I mean, she is in one piece. She's scared as hell, but that's to be expected. She's doing as well as can be expected under the circumstances," he whispered, his tone serious. Evelyn listened intently. "Evelyn...I've known you and your family for many years, so I'm not going to lie to you. We have our work cut out for us," he relayed, breaking eye contact with her. Not a good sign at all. Evelyn threw her hands up to her face and finally let her pent-up sobs escape. "I'm sorry...very sorry. There is nothing we can do tonight. They will be keeping Arianna overnight until a superior court judge arraigns her tomorrow morning. I will be in court at eight A.M. I expect that they will set a very high bond. They are charging her with the murder Evelyn. She was covered in the dead girl's blood," Collins said in a dreadful hushed tone like he had already lost all hope. "Oh God," Evelyn gasped. Things were beginning to spin around her. Her ears were ringing. Her head felt like someone had it in a vise grip. It was all too much. Evelyn's eyes fluttered. "Evelyn? Evelyn, are you alright?" Collins huffed, dropping his briefcase at his feet. Evelyn let out a short grunt. Then she placed the flat of her hand on the pale, yellow, cinder block precinct wall for support. "Evelyn..." Collins grabbed her by the arm. It was for nothing. He couldn't prevent the natural course of things. "Evelyn!" he screamed right before her world went black as she fainted. "Help! I need help over here!"

Evelyn came into consciousness in a cold, sterile room at Lenox Hill Hospital. She rocked her head from left to right as her eyes fluttered open. Panic struck her like a ten-ton boulder. She had no idea where she was. "Uh," Evelyn sighed as she became painfully aware of the bandage around her head. Evelyn lifted one, weak, shaky hand and touched the gauzy headdress. "Mmm," she moaned, she could suddenly feel throbbing around her injury. Next, she moved her head to the left and eyed the monitor blipping an annoying, beep, beep, beep, over her head each time her heartbeat. "Oh God," Evelyn whispered, her mouth so dry she felt her lips splitting as she spoke. She closed her eyes back because the pain of having them open was excruciating. A sudden movement to her right startled her. Evelyn jumped, but she knew that if someone was coming to do her harm, she was totally defenseless lying there all bandaged up and helpless. Suddenly, she saw a shadowy figure come into focus. "Hey…I'm so glad to see you," the soothing voice floated over her. Evelyn closed her eyes for a second and took in Max's sweet voice. She opened them again, wanting to say something but had an immediate lost for words. Before she could say anything to him, Max reached out to grab Evelyn's hand. He gave it a soft, reassuring squeeze to let her know he was there for her. Evelyn frowned because she really wanted to cry. "What happened? How did I get here? What are you doing here?" she finally managed to croak out. Now she was looking at Max, the throbbing in her head seemingly intensified.

"Shhh. Don't try to a' talk. You have had a minor heart attack, Evelyn. They a' called me because I was the last a' person to call your cell phone. Don't worry I told them I was one of your employees…they don't know anything about us. You really need to take care of yourself. This stress is going to a' kill you, Evelyn," Max told her, his tone serious yet caring. Tears immediately welled up in Evelyn's eyes. What if it wasn't for Max? Where would I be…in some hospital somewhere with no one to care for me? She said to herself. She couldn't understand how this man was so good to her, especially after how she had treated him the last time they were together. Yet, her husband was still nowhere to be found. Evelyn squeezed Max's hand with what little strength she could muster. "Thank you, Max," Evelyn puffed out, her words strained under the oxygen cannula in her nose.

"I should be thanking you, Evelyn," Max said, cracking that gorgeous winning smile that had hooked Evelyn in the first place. He really meant it. Special Agent Vargas was elated when he'd received the call from the police to say Evelyn had collapsed at the precinct. Vargas had rushed right over to meet the ambulance at the hospital. He'd been sitting vigil ever since. He had a mission to protect Evelyn now. Losing sight of Evelyn would have been a crushing blow to his case, which he couldn't afford. At this point, he still needed her as much as she needed him.

Chapter Fourteen
Having Regrets

An eerie silence had enveloped the atmosphere of the luxury car as it whizzed down the highway probably well over the speed limit. Even the sparkling afternoon sun couldn't change the dreary, almost, funeral-like mood hanging around the car. Annie cleared her throat, breaking the heavy awkwardness that surrounded her and Shelby. It was all she could do to keep herself from screaming, crying, yelling, and worse…jumping out of the car in protest. Shelby shot Annie a glance out of the side of her eye and gripped the steering wheel tighter. So tight her knuckles paled. Please don't let her start up again. I really don't feel up to this. I should've never trusted her with this secret. Why is she staring at the side of my face like she wants to say something? Please just keep your mouth shut Annie. I'm not in the mood. Shelby said in her head. She was having a hard enough time coping with the situation. Shelby thought Annie of all people wouldn't judge her and would just give her the support she needed at a time like this. Shelby could feel the heat of Annie's gaze on her even more now. She just wanted to pull the car over and push Annie right out the door on the side of the damn road. Shelby kept her eyes on the road, flexing her jaw in anticipation. Annie looked at the side of Shelby's face one more time before she mustered up the courage to speak. Shelby braced herself.

"Shelby are you sure you want to do something about this? I mean…maybe you can come up with another solution. I'm thinking on the lines of adoption or something? Find a nice family that will be private about this. I don't know…something other…than…" Annie asked, clutching her Bible close to her chest. "I…I…just don't agree with killing no baby," Annie finally managed. There. She'd finally said what she had been thinking for the past week. Annie immediately felt like a weight had been lifted from her chest. She would've never been able to live with herself if she didn't at least get that off her chest. Annie believed the life of a baby was sacred. She had suffered the loss of her only child before she started working for the Frankels. Annie had also seen the devastation Diane had suffered when she'd miscarried at least four times after she'd had Shelby. The Frankels had wanted more children so badly, but Diane just could not hold another pregnancy, and Miles didn't want to adopt. Annie knew how precious children were to Diane and how badly Diane had wanted more children. Annie could only imagine that if Diane knew her daughter was going to get rid of a child, how devastated she would be. "I think your mother would just love the baby…really. No one would be thinking about the circumstances Shel…oh how your mother would be over the moon over a baby," Annie continued, choosing her words wisely. Annie felt like this was her last chance to convince Shelby to change her mind. Shelby could feel her chest swelling and heat rising to her face. Her cheeks flamed over red as she bit down into her bottom lip, drawing her own blood before she spoke.

"I have no choice, Annie! What don't you understand?!

There is no way I can have this baby and bring shame to my family. Levi is a married man…he is married…get it! He is married to my mother's friend, and I just can't do it! My mother won't ever know about this…right?!" Shelby growled through clenched teeth as she almost floored the gas pedal in her Porsche Cayenne. "Right, Annie?! Answer me now!" Shelby screamed. Annie shook her head in the affirmative.

"Well then, it's not open for discussion any more!" Shelby said with finality.

Shelby just wanted this day to be over. She wanted to get from around Annie's judgmental words and disproving eyes. The faster they made it to their destination; the faster Shelby could get away from this guilt trip. Annie grunted and began mouthing a silent prayer. That was it! Shelby couldn't hold it back anymore. There was, but so much she could take.

Oh my God, Annie! Praying now! You can't be serious! What has gotten into you!! All of this religious talk! Trying to convince me not to do it! If I knew you were going to react like this, I would have gone to Dr. McClosky's alone! I don't want my mother to know anything, but I don't need all of your Jesus talk, all the way there! I thought you would just understand and be supportive!" Shelby barked, slamming her hand on the steering wheel. She was on the verge of tears now. Her emotions had already been all over the place lately. No one could imagine how she felt being pregnant by a married man who was a family friend for years.

Shelby was annoyed that Annie was putting her on such a guilt trip after promising her that she'd be supportive. Shelby didn't really believe in abortion either, but she figured what other choice did she have. She figured that she had her entire future ahead of her. Having a child under these circumstances was just not how Shelby had pictured her nearly perfect life to end up. Not to mention what her mother and father would say. Yes, they would probably accept it...eventually, but Shelby wanted her first child to be the talk of the town and the joy of her parents' life...not a shameful embarrassment. And Levi... how was he going to explain to his wife and daughter about his illegitimate child with his mistress, who happened to grow up as part of his own family. It was like some soap opera of the rich and shameless. Shelby wasn't about to be a part of that story. Shelby's mind raced with all of these things.

Annie had fallen silent after Shelby's outbursts. Annie knew all too well how tenacious and vituperative Shelby could be when she was upset. Once when Shelby was thirteen years old, she'd gotten mad at Annie and called her a "fat nigger slave." Annie had clasped her hands over her mouth, run into the bathroom, and locked herself in. She had cried for an hour, flabbergasted that a child she had raised had said such a thing to her. It made Annie believe that some adult somewhere had spoken those words in front of Shelby. Annie's heart had been broken into pieces that day. She had thought about quitting, but after Diane found out about what Shelby had done, they showered Annie with apologies. Annie had been given two bonuses by the Frankels just to show her how much they needed and wanted her to stay with the family. The thought of that day made Annie shudder now. She knew all too well how disrespectful Shelby could be when she was upset.

Annie just stared out of the window as the New York City skyline finally began to come into view. They had made it to the city in record time with the way Shelby was driving.

Annie couldn't hear herself think, but she continued to pray in her head. Shelby had turned up her rock music in a disrespectful display of defiance towards Annie. Much like something she would have done when she was growing up. Annie let out an exasperated breath. Shelby veered in and out of traffic like a madwoman now. Annie had to clutch her door handle a few times out of fear.

"Ain't you goin' too fast for the speed limit, Shel?" Annie asked softly being careful with her nagging. She could feel the heat of Shelby's gaze fall on the side of her face again. Annie knew she was stepping on sensitive ground with Shelby, but she also wanted to make it out of the car alive. Annie stared straight ahead; her eyes wide as Shelby continued her perilous driving.

"Now you're going to judge my freaking driving too, Annie!" Shelby screamed, turning her eyes back to the road. "Unbelievable! I so regret sharing any of this with you Annie, I swear!"

Just then the bleep, bleep, bleep of a siren behind them caused them both to look up into the rearview mirror. They noticed the red and blue flashing lights at the same time. Annie began fanning herself as her heartbeat sped up. I told her! I told her to slow down! Oh God, now the police after us. Annie said to herself. If only Shelby had listened to her. Shelby shot Annie a dagger of a gaze. If eyes could kill Annie would have been six feet under at that moment.

"Great! Fucking just great Annie! Now, look what you've done! You nagged and nagged and caused me to get stopped by the goddamn cops! My appointment is in twenty minutes! I really should've done this alone! I can't depend on anyone in my life…not even you, Annie!" Shelby boomed as she eased her car towards the small median on the West Side Highway. Annie just shook her head back and forth. "Oh, Lord. Oh Lord," Annie sighed, fanning herself. She was feeling lightheaded now. She clutched her Bible even tighter. This day had just gone from bad to worse.

Shelby released her seatbelt and leaned into the backseat. She began reaching into her Celine pocketbook to search for her driver's license. Annie looked up into the rearview mirror and saw two men in plain clothes walking towards the car on either side. Annie's eyebrows dipped low on her forehead with confusion. Police officers don't wear uniforms anymore? They sure don't look like the police. They look like they up to something bad…not the police. Annie thought as she continued to peer out the side mirror near her door. The men rushing towards the car seemed strange…not police-officer-like at all. Even their faces seemed too evil to be the good guys.

"Shel…" Annie started, her eyes going around. She wanted to share her concerns about the men, but she didn't have a chance. Shelby turned towards her and jutted an accusing finger in Annie's face.

"Shut up! Just shut up! Your talking and complaining and fucking judging has done enough!" Shelby screamed at Annie. Annie snapped her mouth shut. She had a horrible foreboding.

The so-called police officers split apart so that they could approach Shelby's car at either side. One went to Shelby's window and the other to Annie's side. Shelby went to roll down her window, and Annie kept praying. Shelby rolled her window down slowly, her license and vehicle registration in hand, ready for the officer. Shelby had already decided she would just take her ticket like a champ and hopefully still be able to make it to her appointment on time. She tapped her foot in anxious anticipation.

"Officer…I'm so sorry…I," Shelby began, but her words were immediately cut off. Before she could say another word or react, her door swung open, and she was yanked out of the car like a lifeless ragdoll. "Officer!" Shelby yelled, shocked at the fact that she was being roughed up for a traffic infraction. "What are you…!" she started, but her words were short-lived. "Shut the fuck up," the officer hissed, just as he stuck a gun into Shelby's side. "Don't fucking say a word and don't scream or you die. I will not hesitate to pump you full of lead right here," the officer growled. Tears immediately sprang to Shelby's eyes. This was no ordinary traffic stop. Shelby was smart enough to know that right away. Something was wrong, and these weren't police officers at all. "I have money. My parents have money too. I can get you anything you…," she cried, figuring she and Annie were being carjacked by police imposters. Shelby didn't care how much she had to pay. "I said shut the fuck up," the strange man hissed, his breath reeking of stale smoke. Shelby bit her bottom lip to keep it from trembling. As she was being roughly led away from the car, she heard a low swift sound. It was like something she'd heard on television before. Like the sound a gun with a silencer makes. Shelby whipped her head around so she could check on Annie. She got a quick glimpse inside of the car just as Annie's body slumped over.

"Annie! No!! Annie!!" Shelby screamed, as urine involuntarily trickled down her legs. She couldn't help it. "I said, shut the fuck up! The next time you make a sound I'm going to shoot you right here and leave you to bleed out like a dog," the man clamped on her arm and growled in her ear.

"Mmm, mmmm!" Shelby moaned; she couldn't control her grief. She couldn't believe what was happening to her and she damn sure didn't know why. The other man rushed away from Shelby's car, the newly made crime scene, and hurriedly got back into the police car. He was breathing hard like he'd been running for miles. He unscrewed the silencer from the gun. Shelby could barely stand by the time they got her to the door of their fake police car. "Please…don't leave her there like that. She doesn't deserve to die like that. I'm begging you please," Shelby pleaded, trying to keep her feelings at bay. Just then, a car passed by and blew the horn. The passenger gave the thumbs-up sign to the two fake police that were accosting Shelby. Shelby could not believe how easy it was for these men to kidnap her right on the busy streets with people cheering them on. She shook her head as her arms were roughly forced behind her back as if she were a real prisoner. The man placed Shelby in plastic flex cuffs and forced her into the back seat of the police car. She was sure to all of the passersby on the busy West Side Highway it appeared like a run of the mill traffic stop that resulted in an arrest. "Please…if its money you want my father has plenty. He'll pay anything…please just don't hurt me," Shelby begged in a last-ditch effort to save her own life. Shelby thought about trying to kick the back window of the police car for help, but she knew that would just get her an immediate death sentence. She couldn't control the sobs that wracked her body. She could hear the men speaking in another language. It sounded as if they were arguing with one another. Shelby wondered if they were arguing about whether or not to kill her. She felt the jolt of the car moving as the men drove off with Shelby laying in the back seat. "Ann…ieee!" Shelby sobbed into the seat. "God, please save her soul. I'm so sorry for what I did to you, Annie," she sobbed some more. Shelby knew she had witnessed Annie's execution, and it was all her fault. Shelby could only imagine the fate she'd suffer at the hands of her attackers now.

Chapter Fifteen
Levi Channels His Thoughts

*L*evi drummed the fingers of his un-bandaged hand on the desk in front of him. He looked at his sparkly, diamond, rose gold Rolex impatiently for the tenth time. The watch made him immediately think of Shelby. Regret and guilt trampled on Levi's mood like an army on the attack. Each time he thought of Shelby, his mood shifted. She was the one who had picked out the watch during one of their many shopping sprees. He missed Shelby, but he also missed Evelyn and Arianna too. Levi had been hiding out like a coward for days now. He looked down at his hands again… this time the other hand came into his focus. The large gauze on his other hand made Levi think of Kosta and the fifteen other clients that had contacted him since demanding answers about their investments. Levi quickly shook off thoughts of Shelby; he had long since put Evelyn and Arianna out of his mind too. Things were all muddled up in his head, but keeping his loved ones at the back of his mind was important right now. It was the only way he could operate quickly and without distraction. It was the only way he could make a clean break for the safety and well-being of all involved.

If he didn't leave, Levi knew he would cause everyone

more pain than if he would've stayed around. He couldn't think about anyone but himself right now, it was just best that he not have any contact with anyone. Not to mention Kosta and his threats. Levi couldn't take a chance with Kosta leveraging those threats against anyone he cared about. Levi had purposely ignored calls from Evelyn and Shelby for the past four days. There were at least sixty calls between the two women. A few times he'd been tempted to answer, but he thought better of it. He had to sort things out before he could deal with either of them. Levi pinched the bridge of his nose and let out a long-exasperated sigh. His head ached with a million thoughts coursing through his brain. He looked at his watch again; this time, he didn't think of Shelby; instead, he flexed his jaw and balled his good hand into a fist. The bank president was taking much longer than Levi had expected to convert Levi's assets into cashier's checks that could be converted back into cash when Levi was ready. Levi had always had a good rapport with all of the heads of the financial institutions he dealt with, so he couldn't imagine what was going on. He was used to getting his way with everything; waiting wasn't one of the things he was used to in life. "Excuse me," Levi called to the petite, redhead woman who sat behind a shiny, ultra-modern glass desk right outside of the bank president's door. The doe-eyed girl lifted her head, pushed her stringy red hair out of her face, and looked through the door at Levi as if to say "yes." She didn't answer him, just a knowing gaze in her eyes. Levi locked eyes with her from where he sat. He thought she was cute, not as beautiful as Shelby, but cute enough for a conquest. In his old days, Levi would've made a move on a young, pretty, girl like her. Knowing his reputation, he would've bedded her the same night. Levi quickly blinked a few times, clearing his mind of the thoughts. He didn't have time or the energy right now to even consider having his way with another woman.

"Do you know why this is taking so long? I have a flight to catch, and I've never had to wait this long at any other financial institution...or this one for that matter," Levi grunted, clearing his throat afterwards. He seemed a little more agitated after thinking about how much his life had changed with the blink of an eye or in his case, the click of a computer. The girl stared at him blankly like she didn't really understand what he was asking. "I think this is bordering on poor customer service now. I think I have too much money tied up here to be treated this way," Levi continued pontificating in an annoyed tone as if the girl could do anything to help him. She at least listened and let him finish his lecture. Then she broke eye contact with Levi and started fiddling with her hands. Something about her reaction sent an uneasy feeling over Levi. "Are you just going to sit there or are you going to answer the question...call someone...get up and go find your boss...something!" Levi barked. The girl parted a nervous smile and shakily picked up her phone. It was like she was stalling for some reason. She wasn't responsive or fast enough for Levi's liking. He could feel his blood boiling now. "I can't wait any longer," he huffed. He stood up and found that his legs were involuntarily shaking. His instincts were telling him something wasn't right. Levi hated when he felt nervous. He prided himself on his cool, calm, and collected demeanor. He heard the girl speaking in hushed tones with someone on the phone. Levi could only assume she was calling someone to tell them he was complaining.

"Mr. Becks said he'll be right with you, Mr. Epstein,"

the girl said, her voice a bit too tentative for Levi's liking. The information she provided didn't put Levi at ease one bit. Levi looked at his watch again. He wanted to make sure the girl saw him this time. He adjusted his Ralph Lauren purple label suit jacket and bent down slowly to retrieve his Hermes briefcase. Didn't these people at the bank know how important he was? Levi cleared his throat, something he always did incessantly when he was nervous. Nervous was an understatement for how he felt at that moment.

"I have a flight to catch. I guess I will have to have the bank wire the funds to my account. In which case, Mr. Becks will be picking up the tab for all of the wire transfer fees. We are talking about big money here. I don't know whether you know who I am or not, but,…I'm sure he'll regret having to pay the fees," Levi snorted sardonically, as he walked out of the bank president's office and into the space where the redhead girl sat. Realizing Levi was serious about leaving now, the girl shot up from her desk like she was the toy inside of a jack-in-the-box. She rushed around her desk and stood her ground. Mr. Becks had given her express warning not to allow Mr. Epstein to leave, but he didn't say how she was supposed to really stop him.

"Um…Mr. Epstein…I…um…I think it'll just be a few more minutes," the girl stammered, rushing towards Levi with her hands out. She blocked his path with her small body. "Maybe I can…um…get you a drink of water or a soda. Oh yeah! We have a lunch delivery coming soon…I can get you a gourmet sandwich…those are so delicious…" She rambled; her voice was going high like a dying songbird. Levi used his hand and shoved the girl aside. "Like I told you before. I have to go. I have a flight to catch," he huffed. He was sure something was amiss now. The girl stumbled to the side. There was nothing she could do to keep him there. She was no match for Levi—a man on a mission. "Just a few more minutes, Mr. Epstein!" the frazzled girl called at Levi's back. He just ignored her and kept walking.

Levi rushed from the office space. He contemplated finding the stairwell and taking the stairs, but he knew it would take forever. He was on the twenty-first floor. It was where all of the wealthy bank and investment clients conducted their business. Levi rushed to the elevators and tapped the button. He looked at his watch again. The large beads of sweat that had broken out on his hairline were lined up like ready soldiers. Levi tapped the button again as if that would make the elevator come any faster. Finally, he looked up at the light above the elevator doors. The down arrow on the left elevator door lit up white. The doors dinged open, and Levi prepared to step inside, a short-lived feeling of relief washing over him.

"Ahhh, Mr. Epstein. I'm sorry it took me so long," Mr. Becks sang as if he wasn't surprised to see Levi at all. Levi, taken aback, jumped at the sight of Mr. Becks. Levi eyed the other two men that were still inside the elevator. They watched him too. "I really have to go. I have an international flight to catch," Levi huffed. Mr. Becks walked straight into Levi, backing him out of the elevator. Levi backed up, a bit off-kilter.

"Nonsense. You are almost at the finish line now. It'll only be a few more minutes. We'll arrange a car for you straight to the airport," Mr. Becks said, a silly, nervous smile painting his face. Mr. Becks and the two men stepped out of the elevator together. They let the door close before Levi could jump back inside. Mr. Becks clapped Levi on the shoulder and urged him to turn around and follow him back to his office. Levi reluctantly fell in line. The other two men seemed to disappear in the opposite direction. *Maybe I am being too paranoid.* Levi scolded himself. Just as he began to walk beside Mr. Becks, his cell phone began buzzing in his pocket again. Levi reached inside his suit jacket and retrieved it. He read the screen and his heart rate sped up. Levi knew better than to ignore the call. He cleared his throat. "Hello," he whispered into the phone. Levi felt confident this would be the last time he had to answer this call. "Hello," he grumbled again.

"Aghhh! Help me!! Help me!! Please someone, help me!!" the shrill screams coming through the phone made Levi stop in his tracks. He immediately recognized Shelby's screams. Levi felt like his heart would stop. He clutched the phone so tight the veins in the top of his hand bulged against the skin. "Shel? Shel?" Levi rasped, trying his best not to scream. Mr. Becks also stopped walking in response to Levi's furtive reaction to the phone call.

"She will die if you don't have the money tonight. Then…your wife…then your daughter…and last but not least… you. We are not playing any games with you anymore," a male voice came on the line. Levi could still hear Shelby screeching in the background like she was in a lot of pain. His heart was hammering so hard and fast Levi lost his breath. He actually had to inhale deeply in an effort to get his lungs to fill up with air.

"Please…don't hurt…" Levi blurted breathlessly, but he never got to finish before the line went dead. Mr. Becks was no longer smiling after he'd watched all of the color drain from Levi's face. He stepped closer to Levi, his eyebrows dipping low on his forehead.

"Is everything alright, Mr. Epstein? You look like you've seen a ghost," Mr. Becks asked, looking down the long hallway they were standing in as if he were looking for someone else to be there. Levi felt like he'd seen more than a ghost...the devil himself.

"We have to make this quick...I have to go. There is an emergency...my wife...she's had an awful fall," Levi fabricated on the spot. He was glad he was used to quick thinking and making up lies so fast he sometimes amazed himself. Mr. Becks' eyebrows shot up into arches. He knew right away Levi was telling a lie, but he needed Levi to sign an important document before he could release the money.

"Oh, yes, yes. I understand that things sometimes happen. Follow me," Mr. Becks gasped as he began speed walking back towards his office. Levi wasn't happy to have to return to the president's office where he'd just sat for all of that time. He didn't have time to make a fuss about it. Levi just wanted to take care of his business and get out of there.

Levi's legs were moving, but he wasn't concentrating at all. His mind raced with thoughts of Shelby being tortured, beaten, tied up, or worse killed. Levi suddenly couldn't breathe again. He felt like someone literally had his or her hands around his throat. By the time he made it to Mr. Becks' office, Levi was drenched with sweat. The room was beginning to swirl around him. He loosened his tie and flopped down into the chair. "We will make this quick, Mr. Epstein. You don't look so hot," Mr. Becks huffed out. He slid a release in front of Levi. Levi's vision was clouded now, and he could hardly hear. Mr. Becks seemed to be speaking in long, drawn-out words. Levi tried in vain to steady his hand. He let out a strained gasp; he felt like things were closing in around him. He knew he needed to get his signature on that paperwork, or it would have all been for nothing.

"Are you alright? Mr. Epstein...are you alright?" Mr. Becks called out to Levi, holding out a black and gold fountain pen in front of him. Mr. Becks was just as anxious as Levi to get that paperwork signed. Levi reached out with a trembling hand and grasped the pen. It was taking everything inside of him to fight the neck squeezing, short of breath, feeling that permeated his body. Levi had the pen in a death grip. Now all he had to do was get his hands to cooperate with his foggy brain. He blinked rapidly trying to get his eyes to focus on the paper that lay in front of him. "Are you having trouble? Do you need some water? A doctor maybe?" Mr. Becks asked, his hand on his chest in a clutch the pearls manner. Levi used his good hand to scribble his signature on the bottom of the paper. He'd finally managed to seal the deal. Finally! We got him! Mr. Becks screamed in his head. He looked out of the door at the girl and she nodded. Next, it seemed like things unfolded in movie-like slow motion. Levi could suddenly hear the loud thunder of feet pounding towards him. It wasn't long before he heard the loud booming commands and shouts that followed. "Don't move! FBI!" It was the final signal that all hell had broken loose for Levi Epstein.

Chapter Sixteen
What's Done in the Dark

"Famed celebrity gossip blogger and socialite, Deana Shepherd is finally speaking out on the apparent murder of her daughter, Kris Yunger. Kris, who was nineteen years old, is Deana's self-proclaimed, love child with Living Dead wildman drummer, Kristoph Yunger. Deana broke her silence today with the assistance of her family's attorney. 'My daughter was a perfect girl. She may have had some hard times, but what celebrity doesn't. She didn't deserve to be slaughtered like this…murdered like an animal. The person that took Kris' life will pay with the full extent of the law!' Deana shouted at the press conference she held today in front of her Manhattan high-rise. Shepherd and Yunger's daughter was said to have been found slain in her boyfriend's posh loft in the meatpacking district three days ago. The medical examiner's report stated that the girl died of blunt, force trauma to the head. Police will not release any details of the investigation, but a source inside the department has told news four that the main suspect in Yunger's murder is eighteen-year-old, Arianna Epstein, daughter of famed investment banker Levi Epstein. It is believed that Epstein may have been jealous of Yunger's relationship with Epstein's ex-boyfriend. Some witnesses have come forward saying they saw Epstein try to attack Yunger and the boyfriend at a New York nightclub a week before the murder. Police have not confirmed this information. We will continue to follow the story as it develops. I'm Sue Park, news four."

The huge flat screen that hung over the Italian lacquer accented mantel inside of the Epstein's Park Avenue townhouse blared with the news. Evelyn and Max sat side by side on the plush, suede sofa, in silence, listening to the reporter's every word. Both lost in thought for very different reasons. Evelyn was the first to break the silence, causing Max to jump a little bit.

"Just look at her! A shameless wretch all decked out, makeup flawless talking about her dead child. Does she look like a grieving parent?! She didn't even shed a tear during that entire press conference!" Evelyn shouted, looking at Max, although she really didn't want an answer. Max nodded. "Not one bag under her eyes from so-called days of crying…wearing bright yellow as if she's celebrating! Such a media whore. Who wears bright yellow to speak about the dead! Her daughter is dead for God's sake! I can't stand it! She is all dressed up, model-perfect, holding a media press conference about her dead child? I don't think so! I'm sure this media trounce is to boost her blog ratings and any other way she can make money off the poor dead child. People like her make me sick to my core! Shameless!" Evelyn gritted as she watched Deana and her attorney soak up the world's spotlight. How shameless can she be?!

Max used the remote control and clicked the television off. Evelyn looked at him, tears welling the bottom of her already red-rimmed eyes. "You don't a' need to watch the news right now. You need to a' focus on your health and trying to a' help you daughter," Max told her, grabbing her hand in a strong show of support. He had been so supportive through it all. Between Max and Carolynn, Evelyn didn't know how she would've made it through all of this chaos. They had both kept her sane.

"Oh, Max. It's all over the news now. You saw her! She is relentless look what Deana Shepherd has done… not only on television but in print too!" Evelyn cried as she picked up three tabloid magazines from the floor. Max looked at the covers. ROCKSTAR DAUGHTER MURDERED OVER BOYFRIEND. MURDER AMONGST THE WEALTHY. EPSTEIN HEIRESS A KILLER. Max shook his head in disgust and tossed the magazines aside. He looked at Evelyn with sympathetic eyes. "Do you see what I mean? This is all Deana's doing, I'm sure! There is no way Ari will get a fair trial anywhere in New York City…anywhere in the states for that matter!" Evelyn shouted. Max rubbed her leg; all he could do to comfort her at a time like this. He didn't know why Carolynn kept bringing Evelyn the tabloids and newspapers with her heart in the condition that it was.

"Max…this is all so horrible. I still haven't heard back from our accountant about the bond money, nor Levi. What am I supposed to do to help Arianna? I have no choice but to wait for them for that kind of money," Evelyn sobbed, her chest feeling tight again. She had signed herself out of the hospital against the doctor's wishes to be at Arianna's arraignment. The judge, citing Arianna's "wealthy parents" and her ability to leave the country, set bond at ten million dollars with no reduction and confiscated Arianna's passport. Evelyn had felt like she would faint again when she'd heard the bail amount, but she knew Levi had the money, or so she had hoped. She had tried reaching out to him again, but there was no answer. Max tried to comfort Evelyn now, but there wasn't much he could offer aside from his companionship. He held her in a tight embrace, although he knew that nothing he could do would ever take away her pain.

"Ahem. Mrs. Epstein…you have a visitor," Carolynn stepped into the room and announced, hanging her head like she had walked in on something illicit. Evelyn and Max immediately released each other and moved apart. Evelyn's cheeks flamed over. She still felt an obligation to Levi and was embarrassed for Carolynn to see her the least bit intimate with Max.

"Who?" Evelyn asked, completely caught off guard by the announcement of a visitor. She hadn't told anyone she would be staying at the townhouse. It was one of the homes she and Levi had considered putting on the market after Arianna's stint in rehab. Evelyn had decided then that they didn't need to have so many places anymore. She had hoped it would've forced the family back together, under one roof.

Not many people would think to find her there. Besides, Evelyn hadn't been answering from any of her nosey, socialite friends. She was sure that she would be the talk of the town, no need to feed them information. "Who would know I was here and decide to pop up on me?"

"It's me, Evelyn," Aaron Collins announced brashly not bothering to wait to be announced in. He nearly pushed Carolynn to the side as he forced his way into the room. "Look, we need to talk," Collins said gravely. He held no punches; his face was stony. Max stood up, his body language defensive. He felt like he had to do everything he could to protect Evelyn at all costs. Max didn't trust anyone. Evelyn grabbed Max's arm gently to call him back. Collins eyed Max-like Max posed no threat. He didn't even flinch.

"He's Arianna's attorney, Max. Just excuse us for a minute," Evelyn told Max, patting his hand softly. Max looked at her long and hard. He couldn't be sure that this person wasn't there to do Evelyn some harm. He eyed Collins evilly. Collins returned the gaze. Both men held their ground for a few tense seconds.

"Seriously Max…it's ok. I'll just be a minute. I'm serious, he's an old friend, and I'm fine," Evelyn assured. That's when it dawned on Max. He remembered Collins from the arraignment as Arianna's lawyer indeed. He nodded his agreement and stepped out of the room with Carolynn. Collins looked relieved that Evelyn had called off her muscle-bound pretty boy bodyguard.

"I'm sorry. He is just trying to make sure that I am ok after the other night at the precinct. You understand I'm sure," Evelyn said to Collins with a nervous chuckle. "Please, Aaron… sit down."

"I can't stay," Collins said curtly. He looked at Evelyn seriously, and her facial expression folded into a frown from the previous smile that had painted her face. "What's wrong…what is it?

"Evelyn…I'm sorry to have to bother you at a time like this. I came to tell you that the check for the retainer and the court appearances were returned for insufficient funds," Collins announced gravely. Evelyn's eyebrows shot up into arches on her face. Collins put his hand up before Evelyn could say a word. "I can give you a few days…you know I have worked with your family for quite a few…" he continued, but he was cut short. It was Evelyn's turn to speak now.

"What do you mean returned for insufficient funds?" Evelyn asked incredulously. She had never experienced that before in all the years she had been with Levi. Before Collins could answer, Evelyn was speaking again. "We have plenty of money...there must've been some mistake. You have to be mistaken...you need to check your bank for the mistake. It couldn't have been on our part... no, we have money," Evelyn said, her voice shaking. She didn't even believe what she was saying. She knew that things had been a little rocky with Levi's business. Collins didn't speak. He reached into his suit jacket pocket and pulled out a document that had been folded to fit into his pocket. He extended it from his outstretched hand.

"Evelyn, I don't mean to seem harsh...but I will not be able to render services to Arianna unless..." Collins was saying. Evelyn snatched the document from his hand. Her face was a bright shade of red as if filled with blood. The vein in the side of her neck banged fiercely against her skin. Her health condition was secondary to the issue at hand.

"This is nonsense! Do you know who the Epstein family is?! Do you know what we have?! This is not a fly by night family business venture! This family has generational wealth!" She barked as she scanned the document with her eyes. She couldn't be reading that document correctly. Evelyn's head involuntarily moved back and forth. She didn't even realize she was biting her bottom lip until she tasted her own blood. She reviewed the document again.

FROZEN. INSUFFICIENT FUNDS. SEIZED ACCOUNT. Were the words that stuck out on the document. Evelyn's heart thundered now. She was suddenly freezing cold like someone had pumped her body full of ice water. She closed her eyes to hold back the tears. Evelyn felt like someone had the strings to her life and one by one; they were clipping them with a scissor. She swallowed hard and looked up at Collins.

"I...I...don't understand. What does this all mean?" Evelyn asked the question she knew Collins couldn't answer. It was all she could manage. What else would she say to a prestigious attorney like Aaron Collins?

"Evelyn...it looks like the account has been seized by the federal government and all of Levi's assets frozen. I think you need to call Gus and ask what is going on," Collins said, his words dropping around Evelyn like small atomic bombs. Seized by the federal government! All of the assets?! Evelyn's ears rang with the reality of those words. She had already called Gus Beatty, Levi's personal accountant ten times about Arianna's bail. Gus hadn't called her back, which Evelyn found strange. Maybe Gus knew something like this would happen, and that is why he hadn't called.

"I'm sure this is all some kind of mistake. Gus will get back to me soon, and everything will work out," Evelyn said, suddenly a cheery voice coming out of her mouth. Evelyn plastered on a phony smile. It was the role she'd played for so long that it just came second nature to her now. Act as if this bad thing is really not happening. Smile. Keep up appearances. All of the things Evelyn had practiced over the years.

"You've known Levi and me for years; we would never pass a bad check. This is all some kind of fluke. C'mon you know us better than this," Evelyn said, laughing inappropriately. Collin's facial expression was stoic. He let out an exasperated breath. He really felt sorry for Evelyn. She just didn't get it.

Her life had changed…something she needed to face. And face fast.

"I'll need a few days to arrange another payment. I'll have to contact some of my other resources," Evelyn said mindlessly as she stared down at the document she had involuntarily crushed in her hand. Her mood was suddenly changing again.

"I can give you until Friday Evelyn, but after that, I will have to move on to paying clients. Time is money," Collins told her trying to keep his voice as soft as he could without seeming insincere. Evelyn shot him an evil look. She couldn't believe how fast people turned on you when they thought you didn't have money to pad their pockets. Evelyn shook her head in disgust.

"You will get your money. I will do whatever I have to do to get your money," Evelyn said dryly. "Now you can see your way out. I wouldn't want to waste any of your precious and costly time." Evelyn was done with him. Collins picked up his briefcase and headed for the door. Before he left, he stopped and turned towards Evelyn again.

"I know this may be the last thing you want to hear, Evelyn, but it's just the reality of the situation. You should protect yourself while you can. Don't be caught without some sort of protection like Bernie Madoff's wife," Collins preached. "This is definitely just as bad."

Evelyn shot him a surprised looked. Evelyn opened her mouth to tell him off for the insinuation, but she couldn't get the words out before Collins continued. "Not to sound harsh, but it's the truth. The buzz is that Levi is into something he won't soon be out of…even worse than Madoff. So, a friendly piece of advice…stop living with your head under the covers like you've done about Levi's affairs and your daughter's problems over the years. This is far more serious...even deadly. You will be left with nothing and Arianna will be left in jail to rot if you don't do something now. This one account being seized may just be the tip of the iceberg," Collins relayed gravely. His words seemed to hit Evelyn like an open-handed slap to the face. She flopped back on the couch as if she'd been gut-punched. Evelyn knew that Collins was right. It was time for her to stop playing the victim role and protect herself from Levi, Arianna, and even from Max. Evelyn quickly picked up her house telephone. She needed to contact the keeper of her secret stash account. She had learned more than one lesson while being married to Levi Epstein...but self-preservation and deceit were the two most important.

Just as Evelyn dialed the last number on the telephone keypad, she heard loud voices erupt behind her. Chaotic and loud, to say the least. Now was not the time, Evelyn needed it quiet to concentrate. "Shush, Carolynn and Max...I'm on the..." Evelyn said, annoyed as she turned around slowly to scold them for making so much noise. Evelyn immediately dropped the phone onto the glass bar top where she stood in response to what she saw in front of her. The loud clang sent a chill down her spine, but not more of a chill than what she saw in front of her. It was as if a never-ending line of strange people were rushing at Evelyn. Her head whipped from side to side so fast her eyes couldn't keep up with it. She hadn't seen one face. They were all a blur and so was the situation. "What is going on here?! Who are you?! What is this?!" Evelyn belted out. She was moving fast and furious to stop these pillagers from invading her home. "Don't touch anything! Get out all of you!"

she screeched. Evelyn wanted to grab them all, stop this all-out invasion. Finally, someone stopped in front of her long enough to tell her what was going on. Evelyn's nostrils flared as she looked at the portly, balding man in front of her.

"Mrs. Epstein? I am Special Agent Assisi from the Federal Bureau of Investigation," the overweight man in the dark suit said as he rushed towards Evelyn with his badge in hand. Evelyn's face had gone from burnt red to notebook paper pale. She clutched at her neck as she watched a gang of men and women rush around her home like scavengers on a hunt. Some wore suits and others wore dark jackets with bright yellow letters on the backs. FBI. SEC. IRS. CID. To name a few.

"What is the meaning of this?" Evelyn managed to say to the ugly man. She felt faint again but was determined to stand her ground. "What legal right do you have to be in my home? Do you know who my husband is? His family?" Evelyn said weakly. It was the only defense she could muster. She had hidden behind the Epstein name for so many years that it was unfathomable now that it didn't even matter anymore. The name held no weight. It was a fact that Evelyn was not ready to live with at all.

"Mrs. Epstein, we have a search and seizure warrant for your home. Your husband, Levi, has been arrested. If you want to speak with us, we can go to another room…away from all of this confusion. I know this is upsetting, but we do have a legal right to be here ma'am," a man who called himself Special Agent Kemp chimed in from behind his obese counterpart. "I think you'll be interested in what we have to say…if you give us a minute to explain," he followed up. Levi arrested?! I knew my suspicions were right! Evelyn felt so stupid. So betrayed. She had stumbled across some of Levi's work a time he was on one of his many business trips. After looking over the documents, she suspected that Levi had been lying to his clients about their investment returns. Evelyn had kept her suspicions to herself; she planned to use it as leverage one day. Obviously, she didn't get that chance. Evelyn didn't imagine that it was this bad.

"Should I get an attorney? I mean…my husband…he ran his own business. I am just a housewife and mother. I don't know much about his dealings…or his business," Evelyn lied, wringing her hands together from nerves. Kemp and Assisi looked at one another knowingly. They had been watching Evelyn for months too, so they knew she had more knowledge then she was letting on. Innocent wife, the unsuspecting wife didn't suit her that well. "If I am guilty of anything, it might be shopping. Other than that, I won't be able to help you," Evelyn said, her words rushed and shaky. She wondered if they knew about her secret stash. There was no telling how far the feds had dug into their lives. Evelyn wondered if they knew her daughter had gotten arrested too.

"We can't advise you either way, but we can tell you that we have a legal right to be here. We will be searching and seizing any evidence that relates to our case. And we will be searching the whole house," Kemp said, sounding official and stern. "Now if you follow us to the area, we have set aside for you and your houseguest to sit in while we search," Kemp continued, stepping aside with his hand outstretched like a butler so that Evelyn could lead the way. When she entered the large foyer of the townhouse, she found Carolynn sitting on the small shoe bench Evelyn had imported from Paris a few years earlier. Carolynn's eyes were wide as dinner plates as she looked up at

Evelyn.

"Mrs. E…what's going on?" Carolynn asked, worry furrowing her brow. "All of these police…why are they doing this. It's just so…so scary. Does this have anything to do with Ari? Is Mr. E and Ari alright? Will they be here all night? Can we leave? Did we all do something wrong?" Carolynn shot questions at Evelyn fast and furious like pellets from a toy gun. Evelyn put up her hand to pause Carolynn. Evelyn felt like she was under fire. Evelyn didn't have answers herself to all of those questions. She had no idea what the hell was going on.

"Carolynn…please. Please. I have no idea, Carolynn. I have to sort all of this out myself," Evelyn put her hands up and said in a low grumble as she sat down. Evelyn looked around the foyer and back into the house for a few seconds. She looked over at Carolynn and didn't see anyone sitting next to her. It dawned on Evelyn at that moment that she had not seen Max since the invasion of the federal agents.

"Where is Max?" Evelyn asked, noticing that he wasn't anywhere in the near vicinity. Carolynn's eyes widened again a bit. Evelyn's pulse quickened. Did they take him away? Was he in the country illegally? This would all be my fault. All sorts of things ran through Evelyn's mind. "Max? Carolynn where is Max?" Evelyn said, more frantically now. She was on her feet standing in Carolynn's face now. She really wanted to grab Carolynn's shoulders and shake her until she spits out the answer. "Carolynn!"

"I don't know! They took him inside with them. It seemed like he…he…" Carolynn was saying, but she wanted to choose her words wisely. She didn't want to ruffle Evelyn's feathers any more than they already were, but something just didn't sit right about Max with Carolynn. Evelyn wasn't letting up. She wanted to know everything. Max was the only person she had in her corner right now.

"He what? Took him inside for what?" Evelyn spoke over Carolynn. "What! I want to know what they said to him!" Evelyn pressed, finally following her brain and grabbing and shaking Carolynn's shoulders. Carolynn looked as if she had already said too much. She swallowed the lump of fear that had formulated at the back of her throat. "Well spit it out! What is it?" Evelyn asked, given the look on Carolynn's face. She realized she was scaring the poor woman. Evelyn eased up a bit. "Carolynn it is important that I know where they took Max," Evelyn said as calmly as she could muster.

"Well, Ms. E, I hate to say this but, it seemed like Max knew the FBI agents that came into the house. He…he…just seemed to be very familiar with them. They were talking to him like they'd seen him before. Like they knew him very well," Carolynn finally spit out what she had been trying to say. Evelyn's face folded into a frown. What did she mean he seemed like he knew them! Evelyn twisted her lips as if she didn't believe her hired help. Carolynn had never lied to her before, and there was no reason for her to lie now. "Are you sure? What makes you say that?" Evelyn asked brusquely for clarification.

"I wasn't supposed to be listening, but I could hear Max talking to them. More like arguing with them. He was saying something like…they should have called him before they came here. I swear…it was the strangest thing. He also no longer had an accent when I overheard him speaking with them," Carolynn reported, her words were full of regret. She could see the pain streaking across Evelyn's face. Evelyn was gone from in front of Carolynn in a flash. Evelyn stormed back into the house where the federal agents were still pillaging through her family's things. Evelyn's face was red hot with fury. She wanted answers, and she wanted them now! "Max!! Max!!" She screamed angling around corners and through doorways into the main part of the house. She didn't care that every area of her home was now swarming with law enforcement officers. "Max! Where are you?! Evelyn shouted, garnering a few strange stares from some of the agents. Kemp finally came out of Levi's office where he had been searching, in response to Evelyn's screams. "What's the matter, Mrs. Epstein? Is there a problem?" Agent Kemp asked Evelyn. How dare he ask me if there is a problem while he is rummaging through my home like I'm some common criminal! Evelyn screamed silently in her head. Her cheeks were flushed red; her nostrils flared. She stormed towards Kemp with her eyes squinted into dashes.

"Where is Max?! Why do you have him secluded from me?! What do you want with him?! He has nothing to do with all of this! He doesn't even know my husband! Where is he!!" Evelyn shouted in Kemp's face, her shaky finger jutting at him accusingly. Kemp let out a long sigh like Evelyn was getting on his nerves. That didn't deter her one bit. It was bad enough they'd relegated her to the foyer of her own home, but they were not going to trample over Max too. She wasn't backing down this time. "I demand to know what you've done with him! He is my houseguest, and he should be free to leave! Max! Max!" Evelyn shouted. Agent Kemp put up his hands in a halting motion. Just then Max stepped up behind Kemp. Assisi was right next to Max. Max's eyes were glassy, and his mouth was downturned. "Max! Oh, my God!" Evelyn screeched, a look of relief washing over her face. She opened her arms as she moved towards him. "I thought they had tried to deport you or something awful like that! Are you ok? What did they talk to you about? You don't have to answer any of their questions… you know nothing about any of this," Evelyn rambled, throwing herself into Max. She hugged him hard. He stood there with his arms at his side. It was like he couldn't move. "Max? What is it? What did they tell you?" Evelyn persisted, noticing his body language. She wanted to make sure everything with her and Max was all right. She couldn't stand to lose him at his point. "Max?" Evelyn said with a sense of urgency. Now, the entire room seemed to be watching them. Evelyn couldn't understand what was going on. Assisi stepped closer to them. Evelyn eyed him. Then she looked at Max again.

"Well, Vargas…I think it's time you tell Ms. Epstein who you really are," Assisi said with a snide grin on his face. He clapped Max on the shoulder like a father sending his son into a hunt for the first time. "We'll give you a few minutes to break the news, but don't make it that long. We don't have all day, there is plenty of work to be done here," Assisi grumbled letting go of Max's shoulder and stepping aside. Evelyn's mouth sagged on each side, and she stepped back a few paces so that she could look in Max's face. She couldn't grasp what was going on. More like she didn't want to believe what was happening right before her eyes. Pain shot through Evelyn's chest. She clutched at her collar.

"Wha…what…is he talking about Max? Why is he calling you Vargas? Who the hell is Vargas?" Evelyn rasped out, her words catching in her throat. She could feel tears burning like acid at the backs of her eye sockets. "What does he mean to tell me who you really are?" Her heart thundered against her sternum now. She was afraid of whatever she was about to learn. Evelyn didn't think there was much more she could take. Max reached out to grab her hand, his eyes low, filled with remorse. Evelyn snatched her hand back like he was a venomous snake. "No! Don't touch me! Who are you?!" she screamed on the verge. He moved a few paces away from her. "Tell me!! Tell me, right now!! What are they talking about Max! Who are you?! Why are they calling you Vargas?! Your name is Maxmillion Vega so why are they calling you Vargas?!" Evelyn screamed, tears finally springing to her eyes. She already knew the answer, but something inside of her wanted and needed to hear it from his mouth.

"Evelyn. I am so sorry…let me explain everything to…" Max was saying with his accent completely gone. Assisi pushed him aside. Max stumbled sideways, caught off guard. His hands involuntarily curled into fists. He immediately wanted to punch Assisi in his face.

"Oh, for Christ sake! He is not Max or Maxmillion Vega…or whoever you thought he was. He is Marcellos Vargas, FBI agent…undercover FBI agent! He has been undercover all of this time, and your little boyfriend never loved you one bit. All of the shopping sprees, trips, gifts…that was all a lie," Assisi shouted cruelly. He didn't care one bit that he had just crushed this rich bitch's entire world. Evelyn's head started to spin. Tears were falling from her eyes like a waterfall. She felt humiliated. Embarrassed. Ashamed. Like a fool. She hadn't trusted many people in her lifetime, but what she'd had with Max, in her eyes, she thought was real. It was very real to her. She even thought that she had fallen in love with Max.

"No, see, he was helping us bring your husband down. He just used you to get close...real close. Thanks to you...and Vargas here we have just about all of the evidence we need to put your husband away for years," Assisi continued his cruel rant waiting for Evelyn's reaction. Evelyn swiped at the tears on her cheek and she exhaled a windstorm. Evelyn looked from the man she knew as Max to Assisi and back again. Her nostrils flared in and out as her heart raced. "Is what he just said true?" she asked the stranger she had been calling Max. Agent Marcellos Vargas lowered his eyes, unable to look at her. "Yes, Evelyn... it is true. My name is Marcello Vargas. I am an FBI agent, and I was undercover on your husband's case," he said in a low, sorrowful voice. In a knee-jerk reaction, Evelyn reached out and slapped Max or Agent Vargas across his face with the force of a hurricane. "How dare you!" she spat. "You mean I was your job? A project for you? A case to conquer?! Everything I shared with you was a lie! You used me just like everyone else in my entire life! I hope you rot in the pits of hell for everything you did to me!" Evelyn hissed, the pain she felt almost palpable. Vargas held his stinging cheek as he flexed his jaw ferociously. He never wanted it to come to this. It wasn't supposed to come to this. He was supposed to just disappear from her life one day before they went overt on the case. Evelyn was never supposed to know that what she'd shared with him was all a lie. He knew that would hurt her deeply.

Evelyn shot him one last dagger of a look, then she turned and ran out of the townhouse. "Shit! She's leaving the house! She can't leave the house! This is a controlled environment...it's a safety issue to have her leave the house!" Assisi huffed rushing towards the gaping front door in a panic. Flailing his arms wildly Assisi looked like a man being chased by a ghost. "Hey! Hey! Tell those uniforms to go after her! Follow her and bring her back here! She can't leave until we talk to her! We need her back here right now!" Assisi yelled to some of the other agents posted up outside. "Get her back here now!"

Agent Vargas looked at Kemp and jutted an accusing finger in Kemp's face. "I can't believe what you guys did to me! To her! She is innocent in all of this! You know what she has been through these past few weeks…and now this! You fuckers could've given me a heads up that you were going to go overt on the case today! I didn't even get the courtesy of a fucking heads up! All of this fucking work I put in and this is what you do to me?! Don't you two ever ask me for shit! Get your own fucking clues to where the evidence is…at least that way you can truly say you finally did something on this case besides take a few pictures and fucking get fat sitting in your car! You don't even care about the human collateral damage you have caused!" Vargas gritted, the heat of his breath hovering over Kemp's face.

"It sure seems like someone fell in love," Kemp replied snidely. It was all part of the job. They hadn't anticipated that Vargas might've been in too deep. Vargas stalked out of the house before he ended up assaulting one of his own peers. He had a clue where Evelyn might run. He knew he had to go after her. There were things he just had to get off her chest. He just wanted to tell Evelyn the truth. That he was doing his job and never meant for her to get hurt. This was not how he anticipated his relationship with Evelyn playing out in the end. Vargas knew when he started the case, he'd eventually have to tell her who he really was, but he wanted to do it on his own terms. Not like this. He sped down the sidewalk on a mission. He had to fix things. Make things better for Evelyn. His mind raced with all sorts of thoughts. After all, he had developed feelings for Evelyn whether he liked it or not.

Chapter Seventeen
Behind Bars

The stale air that clung to the cinderblock walls of the jail was like nothing Arianna had ever experienced in her life. It was stifling being there. She never knew she suffered from claustrophobia until now. The cell she was in was smaller than her closets at home. She didn't know how much more of being locked up she could take. Arianna hunched over the small, silver, metal toilet and dry heaved for the tenth time. The muscles in her stomach contracted painfully, but nothing happened. Again…for the tenth time, nothing came up. At least the day before she'd gotten some clear, stomach bile to lurch up her esophagus and spew from her dry, cracked lips. Now, having her face so close to the bowl, the pungent smell of the toilet disinfectant settled at the back of her throat, making her empty stomach feel worse. She plunged her pointer finger into the back of her throat one more time. One more attempt to get something to come up. One more attempt to move her closer to the death she'd been hoping for. Nothing happened. Arianna knew then she was completely dry inside. That's exactly what she had wanted. Weak and dizzy, probably from dehydration, she crawled the two paces it took to get from the toilet back to her hard, metal, bunk. Arianna used what little strength she had left to climb onto the slab of metal. It was covered with a thin, plastic mattress and a ratty, threadbare gray blanket. The smell of the blanket had made Arianna sick her first night there. It was what she would've imagined mildew or mold to smell like if she'd ever had to imagine such a thing.

Arianna's head pounded as she tried to get into a position that was at least comfortable. That was nearly impossible on the hard bed. She grabbed the so-called blanket and pulled it over her arms. The blanket wasn't even big enough to cover her whole body, so she had to choose which part she was going to keep warm. Arianna had seen better blankets in first class on airplanes than they had given her at the jail.

Arianna let a soft moan escape her lips as her stomach roiled with hunger pains. Starvation was no easy way to die. She had never known, until now, what it even felt like to be hungry, much less starving to death. It even hurt to moan at this point. Her head pounded, and her entire body ached. She was sure she'd probably lost more than ten pounds in the last week. Arianna balled her body into a tight knot and rocked back and forth with what little strength she had left. "Please God, just let me die today," Arianna rasped, barely able to get enough air in her lungs to get the words out. Arianna wanted to cry, her face even folded itself into a crying frown, but she didn't have enough water in her body to even make tears. She was angry at herself after realizing she wasn't even good at killing herself. She had been on a hunger strike since she'd been brought to the solitary confinement unit inside of the Rose M. Singer women's jail on Riker's Island. It was taking way longer than she expected for her body to finally give out. Each time the corrections officers slid the food tray into the slot on her door, Arianna would push it back out causing the horrible food (usually thick lumpy, dark grey oatmeal for breakfast; hard bologna sandwiches on stale, moldy bread for lunch, and green slop for dinner) to fall on the floor. The corrections officers always yelled the same thing through the door, "Food down! No meal in cell seventeen! Epstein, you won't get any more food until next meal call!" It was their procedure to make a recorded statement that Arianna had refused the food. They didn't want to be accused of starving her. Most of the corrections officers knew who Arianna was by now. A few of them cursed at her about the food trays because they would be the ones responsible for getting the mess outside of her door cleaned up.

Arianna had also refused to leave the cell for a shower each day. Most times, they didn't force her, but after four days without a shower, it was protocol that an inmate would have to be forcefully showered. It had happened to Arianna already. The officers had stormed into her cell, restrained her, and dragged her into the inmate shower stall where she was soaped up and hosed down like an animal. Arianna had also refused to leave her cell for the forty-five minutes a day they wanted to give her for recreation. She didn't care to see the drab, grey walls of the jail yard. That so-called recreation time was a joke in her eyes. The first time she went outside, she was put into another cage that was open at the top. What was the point? She had asked the corrections officer. It was still a cage. Arianna could see the sky if she looked up, but was still surrounded by grey walls on every side. It was a big waste of time in her assessment. With no contact other than corrections officers, Arianna felt most days like she was going crazy. Arianna just wanted to die as quickly as possible. The last she'd heard from her attorney, he was waiting to hear back from her parents about her bond payment. That seemed like an eternity ago.

Arianna felt herself slipping in and out of sleep now. Did that mean she was dying? She hoped so. She was praying that her body was finally breaking down before her death. When she heard the cell door locks clicking, she knew she was not dead yet. "Epstein! Let's go! You got a visit!" Arianna's favorite corrections officer yelled to her. He was the same grizzly bear of a man that had been guarding her during the day since she'd been there. He'd told Arianna his name was Yusef. He had been the one to explain to her that she had to be in solitary confinement for her own protection because of who her family was and her frequent appearances in the tabloid magazines. If the other inmates in general population had gotten hold of Arianna, she would've definitely been assaulted or worse, just because of her celebrity status. Arianna thought that it was horrible that she was being punished like a mass murderer just because she had been fortunate enough to be considered a celebrity.

"I don't want to see anyone," Arianna grumbled, pulling her blanket up over her head. Her lawyer was the only person who had visited her lately, and he never had anything good to say like Arianna expected. Her mother hadn't even visited her since her arraignment.

"You don't have a choice today. You need to get out of this cell before you wither away. Let's go, Epstein. Up, up, up," Yusef demanded standing over her now. "I'm not going to sit by and watch you kill yourself in here. You have way too much to live for, now come on," he continued. He snatched the ratty little blanket off of Arianna and urged her to sit up. She moaned and groaned, but she listened to him. She had grown to respect him. She had come to know that Yusef's heart was just as big as his body.

"Who is the visitor?" Arianna whined as she stood up on achy, weak legs. She felt winded already. She managed to slide her feet into the horrible, cheap, white jail sneakers she had been issued. Arianna felt like she could barely stand, much less move enough to walk to the visiting area. She was sure she'd faint before she made it there.

"Someone you need to see. At this point...beggars can't be choosers. A visitor is a visitor. Plenty of inmates in here never get visitors. You need to know that you have people that care about you...look at you right now. Half dead from starving yourself. You need this visit today," Yusef said, his tone serious yet caring. It kind of made her want to cry that a total stranger had seemed to care more about her right now than her own father. Arianna had spent nights crying over the fact that she hadn't seen her father at all since she'd been arrested. All along she thought that her mother was the worst parent in the world, but with all of the time she had to think about things, she'd realized both of her parents were just the same. Selfish. "Alright...let's go," Yusuf said, putting the handcuffs on Arianna before he led her out of the cell.

Arianna entered the small, cramped, visit area and looked around for the surprise visitor. She didn't see any familiar faces at first. Just a few prisoners were sitting across from their visitors with sad faces and speaking in hushed tones. The entire scene was depressing. Mother's visiting their small children, unable to have real physical contact with them. Arianna hated this place with a passion. Within a few minutes of being there, Arianna finally saw a door to the left of where she sat swing open. Arianna sucked her teeth and rolled her eyes as she watched her mother stroll over to the other side of the visit table. Arianna immediately looked back for the C.O., but he had already stepped away. Arianna scowled as her mother took a seat. Evelyn's face was drawn tight with concern. Arianna could tell that the way she looked now alarmed her mother. It was the same face her mother had had the night they'd taken Arianna to rehab. Shock. Concern. Embarrassment. Neither Arianna or Evelyn spoke right away. Evelyn broke the silence first. "Ari…what are they doing to you in here?" Evelyn asked, her tone soft. "Are they feeding you?" Arianna stared at her mother through squinted eyes. Her head pounded even more now. The sick feeling seemed a thousand times worse now that she had to sit across from her mother. "I came to let you know that no matter what happens…I will not give up on getting you out of here," Evelyn said. Then she slid something across the table towards her daughter. Arianna looked down. It was a newspaper clipping. Arianna's eyes couldn't help but read what was in front of her.

WEALTHY INVESTMENT BANKER BUSTED IN
CENTURY'S BIGGEST PONZI SCHEME

Arianna read the big, bold letters. She suddenly felt like someone was screaming the words in her ears. The pain in her head increased, and her heart pumped painfully in her chest. Arianna was sure she'd have a heart attack as she let her eyes travel down to the picture under the headline. There it was. Arianna blinked a few times, not wanting to process what she was seeing in front of her. But it was there. Clear as day. A picture of her father in handcuffs. His face clear, unremorseful, pompous even. She stared at his face, his eyes. His eyes were so stony. She could read those eyes so well. She had done it all of her life. Her father didn't have a care in the world, although his actions had probably affected thousands of people. Although his actions had affected her too. Arianna scanned the picture with her eyes. Searching for some sense of sorrow, but there was none. She couldn't see one bit of remorse in her father's eyes. She couldn't stop staring at the photo. Arianna still couldn't produce any tears although she felt some stinging in the backs of her eye sockets.

"Ari honey…I'm sorry to have to bring you this news. I just didn't want you to hear it from any other source. I wanted to be the one to tell you," her mother said. "I am so sorry he let you down."

"What does this mean? What does this mean for me?" Arianna asked, her words being forced out of her mouth. Evelyn closed her eyes as tears drained from the sides of them. She didn't really know the answer to that question. Evelyn didn't even know what Levi's arrest would mean for her, the family, everyone involved. She couldn't even say where she was going to begin to try and put the pieces of her shattered life back together. Evelyn inhaled and came up with an answer for her daughter.

"It means that I am going to do everything in my power to make sure you are vindicated. It means that I will never leave your side while this is going on. Ari, we may not have what we had before, but it is not going to change my love for you. I am not going to let you down," Evelyn said sternly. Arianna hung her head. She shook it back and forth. Things were getting worse and worse.

"How could he do this to me?! How could he leave me like this?!" Arianna yelled angrily. The room was spinning around her. Things were going off-axis now. "I hate him! I hate him for this! I want to die!" she screamed. Evelyn seemed taken aback. She clutched at her chest, her mouth agape. Yusuf appeared behind Arianna within a few seconds. "I hate him! I want to die! I hate him! I hate him!" Arianna screamed over and over, never breaking eye contact with her mother. More than one corrections officer surrounded Arianna now. "Please don't hurt her," Evelyn pleaded. They pulled Arianna up from the chair. She continued to scream as they led her away. Arianna turned one last time and looked at her mother. Evelyn could see the sadness in her daughter's eyes, and for the first time since Arianna had been born, Evelyn felt a deep connection with her child. "I love you," Evelyn mouthed. She could not remember the last time she had told her own child that she loved her. The thick metal door closed behind Arianna. Evelyn stood up feeling stronger than she had ever felt in her entire life. She would do whatever it took to get her only child out of this mess. Even if it meant turning on everyone else around her.

Chapter Eighteen
What a Nightmare!!

etectives Baynor and Ledbetter stood in front of Miles and Diane Frankel letting the words they had just uttered sink in. The silence inside the Frankel's ritzy home was shattered into a million pieces once the reality of what was said finally hit home. "No! No!" Diane screamed as Miles held onto to her to keep her from hitting the shiny, white marble tile in their grand foyer. It was like the detectives had just dropped an atomic bomb in their home. What did they mean they had found Shelby's car and belongings, but Shelby was missing? What did they mean Annie was found dead inside of Shelby's car? Diane had to be having the worst nightmare of her life. It was all too much for Diane to process. Diane had spent the past two days calling Shelby with no answer. Diane had left so many messages for her daughter that Shelby's voice mailbox was full and not accepting any more messages. Diane had never imagined that something bad might've happened to Shelby. In her assessment, things like that didn't happen to people like them.

"We are very sorry, Mrs. Frankel. We know this is hard to hear," Detective Baynor lamented trying to give Mrs. Frankel a few minutes to grieve before they continued with the details.

Miles looked helpless like he didn't know where to begin comforting his wife. Detective Ledbetter wanted to get on with this notification, but he also knew from years of experience that he had to give the grieving relatives a few minutes before he started bombarding them with questions.

"Can we come inside for a moment? We'd like to sit down and talk about some of the details. Maybe get a few questions answered?" Ledbetter asked respectfully. "There is some very basic information about your daughter and the deceased that we'd like to get from you both in order to try and sort this whole thing out," Ledbetter said to Miles. Diane was clearly in no shape to give them permission to come inside the house.

Miles nodded his agreement. He wanted to help the detectives as much as he could, especially if it meant that he would also get some information about his daughter. He moved aside and invited the detectives inside. "C'mon, Diane. Let's hear what they have to tell us so we can get Shel home as soon as possible," Miles told his wife, trying to sound as hopeful as he could. He held onto Diane very tight and led them all into one of the family's ginormous beautifully decorated sitting rooms. The mood was calm. "Will this do?" Miles asked, trying to be hospitable. He could see the detectives admiring the room like they'd never been inside of a mansion before. "Perfect," Baynor answered. Miles opened his arms. "You can have a seat. Make yourselves at home. Whatever you need to know to help the case, we will provide," he told the detectives offering them their pick of a seat. Diane had finally calmed down a bit. Miles sat her down on one of the Italian leather love seats and he sat down next to her. Baynor admired how they seemed to lean on one another for comfort.

"You say Annie was found in Shelby's car? Dead? How? Why?" Diane croaked out. She still couldn't grasp the fact that Annie was dead. Annie had worked for the Frankels since before Shelby was born. The fact that Annie was dead had been all Diane had heard when the detectives first arrived. It had been enough. Annie was like their family. Diane felt sick in the pit of her stomach. Both detectives shook their heads in the affirmative.

"We were so worried about Shelby. We didn't even think about Annie," Diane sobbed. Diane and Miles had been worried when they did not hear from Shelby for a couple of days but assumed she was staying with friends in the city and didn't want to be bothered with them until she was able to sort things out. They thought Annie had gone home to her family for some emergency because that was the last thing Annie had told them.

Detective Baynor let out a long sigh. She never found it easy to make death notifications to the family of a homicide victim. "That is correct, Mrs. Frankel. The patrol cops found Shelby's car abandoned on the West Side highway, and when they inspected further, they found Annie Jackson inside…dead from a gunshot wound to her temple," Baynor broke the news. She tried to sound as official, yet sympathetic as she could. "Oh, my God! Gunshot?!" Diane blurted, shaking her head left to right. "Annie wouldn't harm a fly! Why would someone kill her?! And Shelby?! Where is my Shelby?!" Diane cried. It was all too much to hear.

"Where is my daughter? What do you know about her? You said Annie was dead in her car…but what about Shelby? What information do you have about her?" Miles asked, his voice cracking like he was on the brink. He had asked the questions, but he didn't know if he really wanted to know the answer.

"That's why we are here, Mr. Frankel...your daughter was not in the car. We found her pocketbook in the backseat, but no signs of her. We are guessing that whoever murdered Annie, might have done something to your daughter...taken her or we fear the worse. We have patrol cars out scouring the city for her. We've put out a missing persons alert, but there have been no leads yet," Ledbetter interjected. He wanted to be honest with the Frankels. Things didn't look too good for their missing daughter. Especially because Annie's murder seemed senseless. There was nothing missing from the car or from Annie's purse. Shelby's purse was also in the car. The detectives had already ruled out robbery as a motive.

"It's not looking like a robbery or carjacking...everything your daughter had...money, credit cards, everything was still in the car. Annie Jackson still had money on her person and jewelry as well. Whoever did this...we figure they had other motives. It might've been someone that knows Shelby or Annie. That's why we are here talking to you. We're going to need all of the help we can get if we have any hopes of finding your daughter," Baynor added. "There seems to be no other leads right now." Those words seemed to hit Diane Frankel like an anvil dropped from the side of a tall building.

"Oh, God!!" Diane screeched seeming to come alive. "If it wasn't a robbery by a stranger or a carjacking and it had to be someone Shelby knew, then it had to be her! It had to be her! Oh, God! It had to be her...she wanted Shelby hurt...maybe even dead! She probably wanted to get rid of Shelby! She was so jealous of her beauty! She wanted her out of the picture!

I'm sure it was her!" Diane roared, spewing wild accusations. A sickening hush fell over the entire room. All eyes were on Diane as she moved her hands wildly. Everyone was hanging on Diane's every word. Miles was the first to break the silence. "Diane! Stop! We don't' know anything like that!" he barked. He hated when his wife let her imagination run away with her. This was definitely not the time for her soap opera antics. He looked as if he wanted to slap his hand over his wife's big mouth. Baynor and Ledbetter both looked at Diane with raised eyebrows. Baynor immediately pulled out her writing pad and a pen. She started scribbling wildly like she was drawing a map to some secret lost treasure. "Who? Who would want to get rid of who? Who is this she you are referring to? Who was jealous of your daughter? Of Annie? What are you talking about Mrs. Frankel…we need to know everything," Baynor asked, a bit too much excitement in her voice for Miles and Diane's liking. Miles cleared his throat with a loud "ahem" signaling his wife to keep her mouth shut. He knew she had already said too much. There was no turning back now. Diane would have to explain everything to the detectives. Every embarrassing detail of his daughter's recent mishap.

"Detective, you have to excuse us," Miles tried to sound light-hearted. "My wife is just upset. She is speculating right now. When she is upset, she tends to get a little crazy," Miles said, putting his hands up as if to say calm down and back up. Diane shot Miles an evil look. She was tired of hiding and acting like they had a perfect life. Their daughter was missing, and she wanted to find her. She wasn't about to act as if nothing was going on.

"No! I'm not crazy! I know exactly what I'm speaking

about!" Diane blurted out, backing Miles down. Miles rolled his eyes and flexed his jaw. Diane turned towards Baynor and Ledbetter and spoke to them directly. "My daughter was supposed to be having an affair with a good friend of ours who is married. It came out the other night at a party. His wife had hired a private investigator, and she had pictures. Lots of pictures. Pictures of my little girl and her husband...together. It was a shock to all of us. It was a lot for us to swallow, but I saw the look in that woman's eyes. I have been friends with her for years; I know when she is ready for revenge. That look... it wasn't just hurt; it was anger and disdain for my child. I felt like she wanted my daughter dead!" Diane boomed, her voice stern and very sure of what she was saying. Everyone looked around at one another. They must've all been thinking that was like some wild television show scenario. Diane wasn't about to back down. Miles pinched the bridge of his nose. The other night was something he had tried to put to the far reaches of his mind. Shelby knew better than to mess with a married man. But a married man that was Miles' friend was crossing the line.

Ledbetter moved to the edge of his seat. He had his palms on his knees and his eyebrows furrowed in deep concentration. It was like Diane was teasing them with the information she had. Baynor's eyes were pleading with her to tell them who it was.

"Who is this friend your daughter had the affair with? Who is the wife that you think wanted your daughter dead? Ledbetter finally asked the question that they all knew was coming next. Miles swallowed hard. It had been hard enough for him to wrap his mind around how his good friend Levi could violate his daughter in such a way. Levi had been around since before Shelby was born. Miles hated to have to hear it over and over again. He curled his hands into fists, just thinking about it all. If he could just get his hands-on Levi now, there was no telling what Miles would do. Shelby was his little girl, and Levi should've known that she was off-limits to his sick, disgusting lust. The tops of Miles' hands ached he had them balled so tight. Miles couldn't even speak he was so lost in angry thought.

"Oh, I'll tell you exactly who they are! Levi Epstein is the man my daughter was having an affair with. His wife is Evelyn Epstein. They were people we considered our closest friends! Levi seduced my baby girl, and now I believe Evelyn has done something to harm her!" Diane yelled, interrupting Miles' thoughts. Now it was like Diane was dropping bombs of her own. Ledbetter scrubbed his hands over his face and let out an involuntary groan. Baynor shot up out of her seat like she had been sitting on an eject spring; her heels were sounding off on the marble floors like gunshots ringing out. This was all like one big crazy human puzzle. Ledbetter closed his eyes and let the information he'd just heard sink in for a minute. A more eerie silence settled over the room. Diane and Miles watched both detectives' reactions to the information. It was clear that they knew something that the Frankels didn't know.

"What is it? What is going on?" Diane asked, dabbing at her face. She had gone from sad to enraged now. "What do you know about the Epsteins?" Diane urged, her voice forceful and to the point. Baynor looked at Ledbetter. He looked back at her. With her eyes, Baynor let her partner know that she wasn't going to be the one to answer the question. Baynor's mind was too muddled to think straight. Ledbetter knew what he had to do. He was just afraid of the reaction Diane and Miles might have.

"Detectives? What do you know?" Miles followed up

from his wife's question. He was growing a bit impatient with the waiting game as well.

"Mr. and Mrs. Frankel...have you seen the news these past few days?" Ledbetter asked, looking at them both seriously.

"We haven't been watching much television these days. We have been trying to recover from the biggest embarrassment of our lives. I don't think you understand when we say it was revealed to all of our closest friends that our daughter was sleeping with a married man. So, no we haven't seen the news...what is it?" Miles responded, his face curled into a confused frown. They could all tell he was trying to hold on to his composure. Ledbetter let out a long grunt. It's what he did whenever his nerves were getting the best of him. Baynor was moving on her feet like she couldn't keep still. She had not expected to hear anything more about the rich and shameless Epstein family. This was more than even she had bargained for. Baynor didn't think after the father and daughter were arrested, it could get much worse than that. This new twist had her stomach in literal knots.

"Levi Epstein was arrested by the feds two days ago for running one of the biggest Ponzi schemes in history, and his daughter Arianna was arrested almost two weeks ago for the murder of a rock star's daughter. Things for the Epstein's are pretty horrible right now...so are you telling us that his wife might be a suspect in your daughter's disappearance as well?" Ledbetter announced and asked all in one big exasperated breath. He had to inhale after letting out that mouthful. It even sounded ludicrous to him as he told the Frankels.

Miles and Diane looked at the detective-like they weren't hearing him correctly. Diane's mouth was open, and Miles' eyes were wide as dinner plates. Detective Baynor stopped moving for a few seconds. It was like something had hit her all of a sudden. She didn't even give the Frankel's a moment to react to what they had just learned.

"Mr. and Mrs. Frankel, does your daughter still have a room here? Or do you have keys to her home?" Baynor asked, her mind was racing in a million different directions. There had to be something about Shelby's disappearance that was linked to the Epsteins. Maybe Diane was on to something.

"She had a room here. She's been staying with us since the whole thing with Levi blew up," Diane whimpered. The tears were back. "But I don't have keys to her condo. The keys might be in her purse. You said you recovered her purse, right?" The word recovered made Diane think of a disaster, and she lost it again. She began sobbing uncontrollably now. Miles moved close to her and pulled her into him. He held her close, comforting her. "How could we have been so stupid? How did we miss signs of the affair?" Diane sobbed.

"Can we take a look around? We want to be sure we cover all of our bases. There are just too many loose ends here," Detective Ledbetter came in on the end of Baynor's request. Miles stood up, gently releasing his wife. He looked at her. She nodded her approval. They wanted to do whatever it took to bring their daughter back home safely.

"I'll show you around," Miles said, waving the detectives on. Baynor and Ledbetter looked at each other and exchanged a knowing glance. They fell in line silently behind Mr. Frankel, hoping like hell they would find something that would give them a real clue as to what was going on.

Detective Baynor stepped into Shelby's room and looked

around. Amazed. The room was huge in comparison to Baynor's entire apartment. It was lavishly decorated, pink, black and white. Beautiful silk curtains hung from the five windows that surrounded the room. Custom made for sure. Detective Baynor knew expensive when she saw it. The room had a schoolgirl designer touch. A pink and black zebra print duvet covered the oversized king bed. Posters of boy bands hung on the walls, and fluffy pillows with Shelby's initials covered the head of the bed. Detective Baynor looked around for a few minutes curiously, picking up framed pictures of Shelby and Diane and some of Shelby alone. She really is a beautiful girl. Detective Baynor had to admit to herself. She walked over to the vanity in the far-left corner of the expansive room. All sorts of designer fragrances sat atop the beautiful, white, tabletop. Baynor bent down and picked up a few. She sniffed a couple. "Hmm. Expensive. Everything is expensive," she whispered to herself. After placing the last bottle back down, she stepped away but something inside of the garbage caught her eye. It was a plastic, drugstore bag. Nothing was off-limits. That was what Miles and Diane had told the detectives when they let them into Shelby's room. Baynor grabbed the handle of the bag and pulled it up out of the can. She peered inside and her heart immediately sped up. She turned around to where Ledbetter and Miles were standing talking about some of Shelby's high school accomplishments. "Hey, Leddy...c'mere for one minute," Baynor summoned. Ledbetter excused himself and walked over to Baynor. "What's up?" Ledbetter asked. Detective Baynor held the bag open and didn't say a word. Ledbetter looked into the bag. He scrubbed his hands over his face. "Dammit!" he grumbled.

"Who's gonna tell them...you or me?" Baynor asked.

Ledbetter shook his head from left to right. "I really don't think it matters at this point. Even flipping a coin to choose won't make a difference in how difficult this one is gonna be," he replied. They both looked over at Diane and Miles standing huddled together in their daughter's bedroom doorway; neither one of them wanting to be the one to tell them that their missing and possibly dead daughter was carrying their grandchild.

Chapter Nineteen
Kosta's Stand

Kosta blew the cigar smoke out of his mouth just as easily as he had taken it in. The grey haze from the smoke cast a gloomy cloud over the entire room. The mood in the room was the same…gray and cloudy. Kosta exhaled again. He had to take a few minutes to process the information he had just received. He looked up at his main henchman, Villar, and spoke slowly as if he wanted to emphasize his understanding of each word. "So you say that Epstein is in the hands of the feds now? Arrested? That he was running a scam with all of his client's money? Maybe even my money?" Kosta repeated what he had just been told. Villar nodded, his eyes wide, his heart hammering. All of Kosta's workers knew how unpredictable his mood could get. There was no telling how Kosta might react to this kind of bad news. Villar had once watched Kosta beat a man to death because Kosta lost a hundred thousand dollars on a horse race. This was even worse. Much more of Kosta's money was at stake here.

"Villar…are you saying that all of the money I gave to Epstein is gone? And there is nothing I can do about it?"

Kosta asked. He was asking, but he already knew the answers to his own questions. The words had made the acids in Villar's stomach churn. Kosta's stoic facial expression made Villar ball up his toes in his shoes.

"That's right. I went to see the wife at the police station like you said. The daughter has been arrested for murder. I found out...Epstein has been arrested too. Ponzi scheme they call it. Like Madoff...but worse," Villar relayed carefully. Kosta listened intently as he stubbed out his cigar. He leaned into the mahogany wood desk he sat behind.

"What about the other girl? The mistress," he asked, steepling his fingers in front of him.

"Yes, I got her like you asked. We have her in the van," Villar answered. He nodded at two other men standing posted up near the door of Kosta's office. The men began moving, the rustle of their suits the only sound in the room. Villar looked at his boss seriously.

"Before they bring her in, Kosta, I want to ask...what will you do with her?" Villar asked his boss. He knew he was taking a chance by asking. Kosta shot him an evil glance. Villar felt the heat of Kosta's gaze bearing down on him. Kosta knew that his hired help was trying to make the point, that if Levi wasn't around to pay the ransom for the girl, they would most likely have to dispose of her. Kosta didn't like to be questioned. He also didn't like when one of his lowly workers tried to point out the obvious to him before he could make the point himself. Kosta flexed his jaw.

"Why are you worried about it? You like her or something?" Kosta asked, annoyed. Villar immediately knew he had said too much. He didn't mean to wear his feelings on his sleeve, but it had been hard when it came to Shelby. The day he had snatched her, he later found out exactly who she was and why Kosta had snatched her. Villar had instantly fallen for her. She was stunningly beautiful. Her innocence in all of this made him that much more attracted to her. It wasn't often Villar let himself form any attachment to what he called his "subjects," but he couldn't help it this time. He was human and his attraction to Shelby was instant. That was a big no, no in his line of work. Falling for one of his victims could lead to big problems. Especially if Kosta got wind of it. Villar knew he couldn't look the least bit weak in front of Kosta or else that could be bad news. Kosta always said… "a hitman with feelings is too dangerous. That kind will turn on you in a minute."

"Never! I don't like her! I know better than that! I'm not stupid…I would never fall for one," Villar lied, partially speaking in his language for emphasis. Villar looked away; he couldn't afford for Kosta to look in his eyes. Villar knew that Kosta was very smart and perceptive. Before Kosta could say anything else, the other two men returned with Shelby in tow. They dragged her into the room and closed the door behind them. Kosta eyed her up and down. From the looks of it, his men had treated her decently. Well, as decently as a kidnapped victim could be treated. Aside from a few bruises on her shapely legs, Shelby looked to be in good condition. Kosta could tell that she was afraid. Her entire body trembled like a leaf in a windstorm. They had her hands bound in front of her, and her eyes were covered with a piece of thick black material. Typical. Kosta took a minute to examine her before he spoke.

"Shelby is it?" Kosta said, trying to make his words as plain as possible with his thick accent. He could tell that the girl was beautiful too. No wonder Villar liked her. Kosta himself could see why any man might cheat on his wife with Shelby.

"Yes...that's me! Please! Please! Whoever you are help me! Whatever you want my parents will give you! They have money! They have jewelry! Please, let me contact them! Pleasse!" Shelby pleaded, her voice hoarse from screaming and crying for days now. She didn't know if this would be her last chance to beg for her life or not. Shelby was not going to let this opportunity pass her by. Kosta chuckled a bit. Something about this pretty girl begging and offering her parents money to him amused him.

"Your parents have money, jewelry, and everything? You are sure your parents will save you, huh? You think it's that easy...just give us money and jewelry?" Kosta asked, slightly annoyed by how Shelby minimized their work. Shelby was crying so hard she couldn't answer, but she shook her head up and down rapidly. "I'm not interested in your parents' ransom money! Your boyfriend...he's Levi Epstein, no?" Kosta asked, getting to the point. "He knows you are here, no? My people let you call him, no? Well, where is he to save you? Where is his money and jewelry? Since you think that is what we want."

"No. No, please. Levi...he...he was just someone I was seeing temporarily. He is not my boyfriend! Whatever he did to you, please...it has nothing to do with me! He will tell you...we are not together at all," Shelby cried. It was starting to sink in that her captors didn't care about money. They wanted some kind of revenge on Levi. Her teeth were chattering so hard she felt like her veneers would crack. Kosta laughed at her, but inside he was disgusted. He thought it was so funny how disloyal Americans could be. In his native country, when there was a war, if an opposing faction captured a soldier's wife, she never disowned her own husband even if it meant she would die. If a child was captured, that child would announce proudly who their parents were, even if it meant his or her death.

"You rich Americans will turn against your own quickly, no? Is there no loyalty in this country?" Kosta spat. "Levi doesn't care about you, nor you about him. But you were sleeping together? You were spending his money, no? Ruining his marriage...amazing how quickly you forgot that you were his slut for a long time. You did not care about his family," Kosta taunted. He was disgusted inside with Shelby. If he didn't need her he would've pulled out his own gun and shot her himself. Coming from a broken home because of a father who constantly cheated on his mother with women like Shelby, Kosta felt a pang of hatred for Shelby cropping up inside of him.

"Please mister! You have to believe me! I didn't mean to have the affair...it just happened. I just want to see my parents... please! Please don't hurt me. I never meant to hurt anybody," Shelby begged, her legs were beginning to feel weak.

"You worked for Epstein too, no?" Kosta asked because he wanted to get to the point of his meeting with her. He wasn't done with this little girl just yet, but if she stood in front of him any longer, there was no telling what he might do to her. He knew from watching Levi all of those days that Shelby knew more than she was letting on. Kosta could have easily snatched Evelyn, but he figured Shelby would be of better help to him if Levi had tried anything funny. Kosta had seen Shelby accompanying Levi to several financial institutions. She knew more than she was letting on.

"Yes, I did work for him. I was his assistant. I handled

some of his affairs, but I don't know much. I just always did whatever he told me to do," Shelby said, her words rushing out like a rapid waterfall. Kosta was shaking his head up and down while he contemplated what she was saying. She was finally being honest.

"So you know his banking...his business, no?" Kosta said, more so telling Shelby than asking her. He knew that she knew a lot more than she was trying to let on.

"I know some of it," she lied. She didn't know why she lied at a time like this. It had just slipped out. Shelby had spent months digging into Levi's finances and his business. She knew that he had been in the process of stashing money in offshore accounts and overseas. Kosta banged his hand on the table. He said something in Russian to his men. They moved in on her like a pack of wolves to a piece of meat.

"Owww!" Shelby screeched as she was grabbed by her matted, tangled hair. "Ok, ok! I know a lot. I know a lot of things about what Levi was doing. He didn't tell me...I...I just kind of figured it all out," Shelby relented. At this point, she had to save herself. Kosta's previous scowling face eased into a sinister grin.

"Good girl. No sense in lying to protect Levi. He didn't care about you," Kosta commented. "Sit down here. I want you to tell me everything," Kosta instructed. The men brought Shelby to a chair in front of Kosta's desk and placed her in it. "Take off the blindfold," he said. One of the men removed Shelby's blindfold. Villar looked at her beautiful face and his insides melted.

"Before you tell me what I want to know...I want you to see what happens to people who lie to me in my face," Kosta said. He stood up, pulled a handgun from his waistband. Everyone in the room looked on with wide eyes. Kosta pointed the gun at Villar's head. BOOM! He pulled the trigger and the man's brains splattered out of the back of his skull.

"Agggh!!" Shelby screamed, squeezing her eyes shut.

"Now. As you were saying…Levi Epstein's business. I need to know everything you know. But remember, no lies," Kosta said calmly with a serene grin on his face.

Chapter Twenty
Cosmo's Unexpected Return

*C*osmo's hands shook as he fished around in his pocket for the keys to his house. His return was bittersweet. He was finally able to return to his loft after being banned while the police conducted their investigation. Cosmo thought about the fact that his girlfriend had died right in the loft and he was immediately unnerved. Finally, able to get the key in the lock, he inhaled and exhaled. When he turned the key and pushed open the door, he stood at the threshold with his jaw slack and eyebrow raised into arches. He blinked a couple of times thinking that his eyes were deceiving him for sure. "What the fuck?" Cosmo gasped, trying to take in the disastrous scene. He couldn't absorb it all in one look. It took a few minutes before it all sunk in. The police and crime scene technicians had made a complete mess of Cosmo's once posh, famously decorated place. The beautiful, expensive Italian leather sofa was turned over on its back, the cushions tossed on the floor in opposite directions like garbage. Black fingerprint powder stained the white leather of the sofa. The glass coffee table that Cosmo had been so proud of when he purchased it was shattered on the top and had the same black powdery residue all over it. His ultra-modern egg white lacquer barstools were turned over, and one was even missing a leg. The floor where Kris had been laying was still stained with dark, burgundy bloodstains. White tape in the shape of her body outlined the place where she had been found. There was police tape, boot marks, and papers everywhere in the loft. The drawers and cabinets in the kitchen were all opened with the contents spilled out onto the counters and floors. Cosmo's expensive artwork had been pulled off the walls and tossed aside like trash. One expensive painting was even ripped in the middle. Not one thing in the loft was left in its place. Cosmo stepped further inside of what used to be his beautiful home, disgusted. Glass crunched under his feet as he kicked his way through the debris, trying to decide where he was going to start to clean up first. Cosmo picked up one of his framed pieces of art and tried to brush it off.

"Fucking cops. And they say we act like animals. Look at what they did to my fucking place. I should sue the fucking city for damaging my shit. Don't they know how hard I had to work to get all of this," Cosmo mumbled as he began trying to pick other things up. He was so lost in thought that he didn't even realize he was being watched. Cosmo bent down to pick up another shattered picture frame from the floor, but the crunch of glass behind him caught his attention. He whirled around on the balls of his feet. He was already paranoid. Cosmo jumped fiercely.

"Don't even think about going for that little piece you keep in your boot," a strange male voice said calmly. "Put your fucking hands up over your head where I can see them."

Cosmo's eyes almost popped out of his head as he stood face to face with the end of a chrome .50-caliber desert eagle special. He felt like his bladder would involuntarily release at any moment. Cosmo raised his hands slowly like he was told.

"Look, man…take whatever you want…I got money in my pocket and in the safe in the room," Cosmo told the man, his voice shaking like a coward. Cosmo looked at the man, with his long blond hair pulled back in a ponytail, his rugged, unshaven face had pegged him as a biker gang member. The man's clothes told it all, a letter jacket, leather motorcycle boots, ripped jeans. A meth headbanger! Cosmo screamed inside his head. He could come up with no other reason for the man to be in his home, threatening him except robbery.

The man reached down and took the small .22 Cosmo had stashed in the side of his boot. He ran his free hand around Cosmo's waistband after. For a meth head, the man was surely operating like a cop or some kind of law enforcement.

"I'm clean man…I ain't got nothing else on me. Whatever you want…just take it. I got some new meth right there in my pocket, just take it. It's like nothing you've never experienced before, and I'm telling you, that you can have it," Cosmo said again, a bit more urgency lacing his words. That was one of the perils of being a two-bit drug dealer. People in the streets always wanted what you had and vice versa. Cosmo knew he was a target for robbery when he was on the streets, but he never suspected that someone would find him at home.

"Oh, you think I'm here for your meth? I look like a meth head to you?" the man asked, annoyed. Cosmo took that back. The man didn't really look like a meth junkie. He actually kind of resembled a model type.

"You look like a biker boy. I'm just trying to figure this thing out man…what can I do for you?" Cosmo said, trying to get to the bottom of this invasion. He just wanted to get out of it in one piece.

"I'm here about the girls…you know the dead girl and the girl that's about to lose her freedom for a crime she didn't commit. I heard you were the state's main witness in the murder case," the man said calmly. Cosmo shook his head back and forth, rapidly saying no.

"Me? No man. You got the wrong person. I'm not a snitch. I told those fucking detectives I don't know what happened here the night of that murder. I left the two bitches here. I told those pigs that. I wasn't here at all man," Cosmo rambled his lies spewing like hot lava from a volcano. The man chuckled at Cosmos responses with his gun still trained on Cosmo's head. "You gotta believe what I'm saying. I'm from the streets I would never snitch on anybody. I don't know who killed the girl but it wasn't me. I'm not working with the police look at what they did to my house! You think I will work with them after this, hell no!" Cosmo said more urgently. He thought his street credibility was enough to convince one of his own that he was a good guy.

The man looked at Cosmo with a smirk on his face. He had just followed Cosmo from a meeting with the dead girl's mother. Not only was Cosmo agreeing to testify against Arianna Epstein, but he was also being paid by Deana Shepherd, mother of the dead girl, to embellish the story so that there would be no doubt a jury would convict Arianna. The man was growing slightly impatient with Cosmo's lies. He lifted the gun and brought it down on Cosmo's head. "Aggh!!" Cosmo cried out. "Please… what do you want man? Who are you?" Cosmo panted, holding his bleeding head.

"I don't have to believe anything you say. In fact, I don't

believe anything you say. In my eyes, you are as low as they come. Two girls have lost their lives because of you. So, I just came to make sure that you won't be able to ruin any more lives," the man announced. Cosmo put his hand in front of his face and examined the dark red blood running out of his head. Cosmo could see the look in the man's piercing blue eyes. It was cold and calculating.

"C'mon man…you gotta believe me. I am a lot of things, but I'm not a snitch, and I'm not a murderer," Cosmos said sincerely. "Don't do this. Just listen to what I have to say… I'm not snitching on anybody." The man didn't seem fazed by Cosmos fake attempt at sincerity.

"Oh yeah, well I think you're lying. I think you got paid to be a witness against Arianna Epstein. You know what else you are not going to do?" the man asked Cosmo. Cosmo just stared at the man. He didn't know the answer to the question, and he didn't want to take a chance by saying the wrong thing.

"What?" Cosmo eked out.

"You are also not going to be alive anymore either," the man said as he raised his gun towards Cosmo's head and pulled the trigger. BOOM! Cosmo's body shrank to the floor like a deflated balloon. There would be no testifying against Arianna Epstein. It was the least Marcellos Vargas could do for Evelyn after the pain he'd caused her in the name of justice. He knew how to commit a clean murder, and it was the last thing he did before he shed his FBI credentials and badge once and for all.

Chapter Twenty-One
What Else Could Go Wrong?

*L*evi could smell his own body odor so strongly now his stomach did flips. He smelled like a combination of must and stale mold like the inside of the jail. He hadn't been able to change his clothes or wash since his arraignment. Levi had made several phone calls since his arrest; none had been answered. He had held out hope that Gus or even Evelyn would come to his rescue. He sat on the hard bench with his face in his hands. "Epstein!" Levi popped his head up and jumped to his feet when he heard his name being called by the jail guards. He hadn't slept at all in the days since he had been arrested, so his head pounded from exhaustion. "Let's go, Epstein. Someone posted your bond this morning. Let's go," the corrections officer grumbled. The word was out around the jail about Levi and how many victims he'd left in the wake of his schemes. There were movie stars, movie directors, wealthy bankers, and businessmen who were all faced with the threat of losing everything. They had entrusted their entire fortunes to Levi.

When Levi heard that his bond had been posted a warm feeling came over his body. Days earlier he was even surprised that the judge had given him a bond at the arraignment. Now,

Levi recognized the feeling that enveloped his body as pure relief. He knew his friends and family wouldn't have let him down, no matter how much he had done them dirty. Levi's heart rate sped up with excitement at the thought of getting out of that hellhole. Immediately he wondered who would be waiting for him outside of the metal doors of the jail. First, Levi thought about Gus, his accountant, but his last conversation with Gus hadn't gone so great. Gus had figured things out a long time ago, and when he had confronted Levi, things had gotten heated. It can't be Gus. Levi surmised. There was only one other person that would care even one bit about Levi. He concluded quickly that it had to be Evelyn that had bailed him out, who else would care enough. His parents had cut him off years ago. In fact, they were the reason Levi had resorted to the criminal activity that ultimately landed him in this predicament.

Levi felt powerful as he headed out of the cell. In Levi's assessment, wealthy people always got a chance to bond out. Levi's bail was set at five million dollars, which would've been five hundred thousand in cash. Levi gathered up the newspapers he'd collected since his arrest. He had to admit to himself that he was secretly proud of gaining his celebrity back, although it was for other than savory reasons this time. Levi had missed being the most popular man in New York like when he was younger. It made him slightly egotistical that he was on the front page of almost all of the newspapers and tabloids in the city. "You were collecting pictures of yourself, huh?" the officer asked Levi with a hint of sarcasm. Levi turned to face the officer with a smug smirk on his face. Even now, as an inmate, Levi felt superior to even the guards and everyone else around him.

"You'll be back. Next time it will be after your trial,

so you won't be smiling like this. I'm sure. Same things that make you laugh will make you cry. Next time, I'll be the one smiling...trust me," the officer commented as he handcuffed Levi to lead him out of the jail cell. Levi didn't even comment. He had no time to argue with the likes of a jail guard. Levi was an Epstein, and he had a higher place in the world. Besides, coming back to jail wasn't an option in Levi's mind. He had other plans. Or so he thought.

Levi was led, in handcuffs, to the processing unit for out-processing. He couldn't wait to be free. He felt like an animal the way they treated him inside those walls. The whole time he walked through processing, Levi was lost in thought about what he would say to his wife. After everything that had happened. After how low Levi had stooped with this last affair, he still couldn't believe that Evelyn would come to his rescue. Levi was glad that she had been smart enough to find the hidden money too, because from what he knew, after his arrest, the feds had seized everything that was the least bit transparent. Now his mind raced with questions. What could he possibly say to Evelyn that would suffice? Levi silently rehearsed the things he would say. Evelyn, you don't know how much I regret the past. I am going to be a better man. Levi shook off those statements because she had heard them all before. Just plain old sorry was the next thing that came to mind, but he knew that was such a cop-out. Levi had said sorry to Evelyn so many times over the years that he was one hundred percent sure that she would spit in his face if he said that. Levi would have to do something so different from his regular self that Evelyn would be convinced that he meant what he was saying. He knew! He had an idea! This time he would get down on his knees and beg her forgiveness for what he had done. That was his plan. He would wait until they got outside to their waiting car, and he would beg her forgiveness. He would grab her for a tight embrace and long kiss, and he would beg for her forgiveness.

"Move along Epstein. Let's go...we ain't got all day," another corrections officer boomed, startling Levi out of his daydream. Levi stepped up to a table where his things were laid out in front of him. The officer was sorting things out in front of Levi, and he didn't even bother to make eye contact with Levi. "One gold Rolex brand men's wristwatch! One black, leather wallet with the word Hermes imprinted on the front! Ten one-hundred-dollar bills! One black, leather men's belt with Yves Saint Laurent imprinted on the inside! Two gold-colored cuff links with white stones!" the corrections officer shouted out all of Levi's belongings one by one. Levi seemed proud of his collection of premier designer things. He knew those jail guards couldn't even afford to have his belt. He felt superior. He was brimming inside with anticipation and anxiety. "Is this all of your belongings?" the officer asked. Levi could care less about the stuff. There was plenty more where those came from. If he had it his way, he would've left every single thing right there. Levi shook his head in the affirmative. The officer slid a piece of paper in front of Levi and without even reading it; Levi mindlessly scribbled his signature on the bottom of the paper.

"Well, mister rich and shameless, I guess you've been bonded out. We will see you after the trial. Trust me; it will be our pleasure to have you back," the correction officer said snidely, spreading an evil grin across his box-shaped face. Levi wondered why the officers all kept saying they expected to see him after the trial. What if he beat the case? They obviously had read too much of the media's take on his so-called crimes.

"You're right about one thing. I am rich and shameless, so when I beat this case with my high paid attorneys, I'll be sure to send you a little note that says kiss my ass," Levi replied, the heat of satisfaction settling over him like a warm blanket. He grabbed his things and walked through the iron doors. Levi had a big, winning smile plastered across his face when he entered the big empty room. He looked as if he had aged ten years in three days, but that didn't stop him from smiling from ear to ear. He could hardly wait to see Evelyn's face. He would make it all right once he was face to face with her. Levi looked around; he didn't see her. Levi furrowed his eyebrows in confusion. He turned back around to ask the corrections officer where his wife was, that's when he heard a voice from behind him. It sent chills down his spine.

"Levi! I've missed you so much! Oh my God, I'm so happy to see you again," the female voice cried out from behind him. The familiar voice was like nails on a chalkboard in Levi's ears right now. It was definitely not the voice he expected or even wanted to hear right then. Levi whirled around on the balls of his feet so fast he was almost knocked off balance. His heart was thundering, and sweat immediately broke out all over his entire body. "Shelby?" Levi said, a halfhearted nervous smile on his face. He didn't have time to look at her good. She was like a blur of blonde hair and gangly arms; she rushed into him and threw her arms around his neck. Levi swallowed hard and tried to return her embrace, but his arms felt weak. His mind raced in a million directions. Shelby wasn't supposed to be there. No! It was supposed to be Evelyn! How could Shelby possibly be there?! The last time Levi had spoken to her, she was screaming on the other end of the phone. Levi was sure the Russians had her. He was contemplating her ransom when he'd been arrested by the federal agents. He had thought about her, but never like this. Levi had to sort this all out. He couldn't even return Shelby's embrace; he was too nervous.

"Aren't you glad to see me? Aren't you glad I'm alive and that I came to get you out?" Shelby pouted as she released her grip on Levi. She wanted to slap the shit out of Levi. It wasn't at all lost on her that, if it were up to Levi, she would be dead at the hands of Kosta. Levi didn't even ask her if she was ok. The fucking nerve of him! Something inside of her still felt love for Levi too.

Levi laughed nervously. Looking around. He could smell a setup. He wasn't stupid...how would Shelby have enough money to bail him out?

"Of course, I am happy to see you, Shel...it's just...the last time. Oh, forget it. I am happy to see you," Levi lied, trying to stave down his nerves. His hands trembled as he finally took a good look at Shelby. She didn't look well. Although she had on makeup and nice clothes, her face looked sunken in. Her eyes were dark, sad. Something about her facial expression didn't sit right with Levi. Her entire appearance...the entire scene...it all seemed somehow staged. His gut ached with the notion that something was not right.

"Let's go home, Levi. We can catch up on everything. We can exchange our stories once we are all alone" Shelby said, her words were robotic-like she'd rehearsed them. She started walking towards the exit. Levi reluctantly followed her, feeling like impending doom. What other choice did he have at this point? He reasoned with himself. It was either follow Shelby or go back to jail. Levi's legs felt like two lead pipes as he walked along. Each stepped labored as if he knew he was about to walk into danger. Shelby's heels clicked-clacked against the concrete floors, each bang seemingly signaling the dread that was to come. When they reached the door, Levi stopped walking. His underarms were drenched with sweat and his stomach in knots. Shelby sensed his hesitation, and she turned around to see what was the problem. She arched her eyebrows at him.

"What is it, honey? You can't be nervous about coming home to me," Shelby said, her voice phony and cracking. She looked like she couldn't take it anymore. Shelby swallowed hard and moved her head from left to right. It was as if she was saying sorry to Levi with her eyes. Her face folded into a frown. Levi figured it out! She was trying to tell him something without saying it. Levi looked at her seriously. Shelby shook her head some more, and tears finally dropped from her eyes. She didn't say another word. She could no longer look at Levi. Shelby abruptly turned around and pushed open the door. That was the signal. It had all gone according to plan. Her heart jackhammered against her sternum as she stepped aside. She silently mouthed the words, "I am sorry." Just then, two men rushed through the doorway and roughly grabbed Levi on either side. "Wait!" Levi grumbled. "Shel," he started. He felt the gun suddenly being jammed into his side. Levi tried to struggle, but when he looked out of the door, he also saw the gun that had been put against Shelby's head. He knew that if he screamed for help or put up a fight, they would kill Shelby right on the spot. Levi relented. Shelby didn't deserve to die like that because of his mistakes.

"I can walk! I will walk to the car!" Levi growled, trying

to show a last-ditch display of toughness. He had to go out with some kind of pride. The two men let him loose. He straightened out his clothes and flexed his neck. One of the men pushed him forward, urging him to hurry up. "Don't try anything funny or the girl is as good as dead," the man hissed. Levi was led to a darkly tinted Mercedes S550. The back door flung open to invite him in. Levi was forced into the back of the car. When he looked over, he almost fainted. Levi felt vomit creeping up his esophagus, but there was absolutely nothing he could do now but face his consequences.

"Epstein. You don't look so happy to see me," Kosta said, followed by a hearty, maniacal laugh. Levi swallowed hard. He opened his mouth to speak, but Kosta put his hand up.

"No words you can say will suffice. All you should say is thank you to me for bailing you out of that hellhole. Other than that…your words mean nothing to me anymore," Kosta droned, blowing out his signature cigar smoke. Levi felt like his throat would seize at any minute.

"Kosta…I…can…I can explain everything to you," Levi stammered, sweat dripping down the sides of his face now. Kosta laughed. "You look like you are nervous to see me instead of happy to see me," Kosta said. Then he snapped his fingers, signaling his men. Suddenly the car was moving. Levi balled his hands into fists so tight his fingernails burned the insides of his palms. Levi's eyes stretched to their limits. He had no idea what was going to happen next.

"If you just give me one more chance. They are mistaken…those things they said I've done. None of that is true. Kosta…if you just give me some more time. I really can explain," Levi stumbled over his words. His groveling disgusted

Kosta to no end. He expected the great Levi Epstein to have some kind of bravado. Some kind of pride. Kosta thought of Levi as less than a human being. Less than an animal even. Kosta looked at Levi with deadpan, disgusted eyes.

"Your time to explain is up Epstein," Kosta said calmly. Kosta raised his left hand slowly.

"Please!" Levi managed, throwing his hands up in defense. Next, his world went black.

Chapter Twenty-Two
The Domino Effect

The interior of the Epstein penthouse seemed hollow, empty, and dreary. The federal agents who'd executed their search warrant at the penthouse had all but destroyed everything inside. Evelyn had cried for days after she saw the damage. They had seized everything of value from the inside. All of Evelyn's expensive china and silverware…family heirlooms that the Epsteins had passed down to her on her wedding day were gone. One of Evelyn's entire collection of vintage Chanel handbags; probably valued at over ninety thousand dollars, was also gone. All of the antique artwork that Evelyn had collected during her and Levi's trips around the world had all been either seized or damaged. The reality of what they'd done had literally taken Evelyn's breath away when she'd arrived at the penthouse and found it in that condition. That first night, she'd drank herself comatose. She'd awaken on the floor with a horrible headache. That was when Evelyn remembered what she had come to the penthouse for in the first place.

Now, Evelyn gathered the last of her stash and tucked it into her oversized Louis Vuitton luggage tote. She inhaled and exhaled the experience was so final, so exasperating. Evelyn stood in her daughter's old bedroom, and she felt her chest tighten. It had been there that she had rocked her only child to sleep. It had been there that she had read her daughter stories and given her some of the finest gifts. That room held so many memories that they made Evelyn's head swirl. The room also held the most important thing that Evelyn would ever hide there.

Taking one last look around Arianna's room was bittersweet. It was so final for Evelyn that she couldn't help the tears that welled up behind her eyes. Carolynn stepped into the room. She had tears in her eyes, as well. It was bittersweet for her too. The reality of the situation had finally settled in on Carolynn. Evelyn turned around to meet her gaze. Evelyn smiled weakly.

"Oh, Carolynn. I'm so sorry about all of this. You have been the best addition to our family. More than I could have ever dreamed of when we hired you," Evelyn said sweetly, tears flowing down her face now. Carolynn dabbed at her eyes. She didn't know what she'd do without the family.

"I didn't get a chance to see Ari after she got home from rehab. I feel so badly that I didn't go after her. I should have followed her and maybe none of this would've happened," Carolynn sobbed.

"No! Carolynn, you stop it! None of this is your fault!" Evelyn chastised through her own tears. She grabbed Carolynn by the shoulders. "You did all that you could do for Ari. I am forever grateful."

"It's just that all of these bad things happened and I didn't even go see her in jail. I feel so badly, but I need to see her before I leave. Please let me come with you to say my goodbyes. I know she would want that," Carolynn implored.

Evelyn didn't think it was such a good idea, but she also felt horrible about what Carolynn had been put through at the hands of her family.

"Ok. You can go with me to bail Arianna out. But after that, we will be going to a location where no one will be able to find us until her trial begins. Ari deserves a little peace of mind. Everything that she has been through is my fault. I owe her that much," Evelyn told Carolynn.

"Oh, Mrs. E, thank you! I will say my goodbyes and say a prayer for you both," Carolynn agreed, her face lighting up.

"Ok. Well, we've got to go quickly. I don't want any more unexpected surprises and everything I do is under watch now. They followed me here. I'm sure they are somewhere close," Evelyn explained as she picked up her oversized bag containing Arianna's bail money. It was the last of everything they had. Every dollar Evelyn had left was inside of that bag. She felt grateful to even have that.

Years ago, Evelyn had taken to stashing bundles of cash in a safe she'd had installed behind a Van Gogh painting that hung in Arianna's bedroom. It was Evelyn's secret stash. A stash that she never really imagined that she'd need, especially not for something like this. Evelyn was so glad she had had the foresight to put something away. Originally Evelyn started stashing the money after she had seen one of her friends get nothing during divorce proceedings with her husband who had secretly tricked her into signing a prenuptial agreement. After she saw her friend so devastated the woman was forced to live in a shelter, Evelyn began putting as much money as she could get her hands on without raising red flags in Levi's eyes away. Evelyn had told herself that she would one day give the money back; that the money was there just in case the Epsteins had ever decided to turn their backs on her like they'd been famous for doing to some of their own family members. But after Levi began his affairs, Evelyn stashed more and more of the money as a safety net for herself and her daughter. Evelyn was smarter than Levi had ever given her credit for in the years they'd spent together. Evelyn wondered if he had a stash somewhere in the penthouse that she didn't know about. She didn't have any more time to look; she wanted to get away.

"Mrs. E, the car is outside," Carolynn announced. It would be the last time Carolynn would tell Evelyn those words. That was a sobering reality that trampled all over Evelyn's mood. Evelyn turned around with tears in her eyes. She was prepared to walk away from life as she knew it. She stepped out of Arianna's room and pulled the door shut behind her. Carolynn waited for her. They smiled at one another and walked out of the penthouse for good. When the door slammed behind them, Evelyn closed her eyes and paused for a minute. "Goodbye," she mouthed silently. Carolynn did the same.

Evelyn stopped at the front desk of the building she'd lived in for so long. She thanked her doorman and the building staff. They all gave her hugs and they were all sorry to see her go. Evelyn cut their goodbyes short; she didn't need any long goodbyes. She wanted to regain her pride and strength.

Evelyn rushed out of the building to the awaiting hired taxi. A taxi was something Evelyn hadn't taken since her days as a starving model just starting out in New York. Evelyn looked at the old, black, Lincoln Town car and told herself it was something she would have to get used to—living like a regular person. It was a far cry from the privately-owned Bentley she was used to being driven in. She inhaled the New York air one more time. She just loved New York, but Evelyn knew she couldn't stay there. Evelyn set her leg to climb into the taxi when she heard it. She stopped cold in her tracks.

"Mrs. Epstein! Mrs. Epstein! Wait! Stop! Police! Loud screams came from Evelyn's left. Evelyn stood back up and whirled around on her feet. Her face curled into a confused frown. Carolynn looked surprised as well. Not again! Evelyn thought as she saw Detectives Baynor and Ledbetter rushing towards her. Evelyn's face went stony. She flexed her jaw. What do they want! I have nothing to say to them! Evelyn said in her head as she eyed the detective evilly.

"Mrs. Epstein!" Detective Baynor said breathlessly as she got right in front of Evelyn. Baynor looked disheveled. She had big bags under her eyes like she hadn't slept in days. Her hair was bushy, and her clothes looked like she'd had them on for weeks.

"How can I help you, detective?" Evelyn said dryly, still clutching the bag that contained the key to her daughter's temporary freedom. She eyed the detective up and down. Evelyn didn't like the woman. It was that simple. She saw Baynor as her enemy.

"I don't know if you remember me! I am a detective…" Baynor was saying, as she pushed her wild mane of hair out of her face. Baynor looked like she was on a mission.
"Of course, I remember you! How could I forget the person that wants to put my daughter away for the rest of her life for something she did not do!" Evelyn growled. "What do you want?"

"Well, Ms. Epstein. We are not here to speak to you about your daughter this time," Baynor huffed. Detective Ledbetter stepped up to where the two women stood facing off.

"Mrs. Epstein. We need you to come with us down to the station. We need to speak with you about the disappearance of Shelby Frankel and the murder of Constantine Sipriano, who you may know as Cosmo," Ledbetter said, his tone serious and demanding.

Evelyn looked like she'd seen a ghost. The detectives watched as the color drained from Evelyn's face. The disappearance of Shelby and murder of Cosmo? She replayed the words in her head. Evelyn felt like smiling as neither one of those facts made her sad at all.

"Yea, we thought you'd have that kind of reaction. We advise you to come with us, Mrs. Epstein. We know that Shelby was having an affair with your husband and that you made some pretty serious threats against her in front of a party filled with witnesses. We also have surveillance tapes from Cosmo's building, and we think you might have had contact with the man we saw leaving around the time we think Cosmo was murdered," Detective Baynor said. It was like he was dropping bombs on Evelyn.

"No! I...I...have nothing to do with any of that. I don't know anything about Shelby disappearing. I don't even know who Cosmo is. I have to go get my daughter," Evelyn said helplessly.

"I don't think so, Mrs. Epstein. Please don't make this harder than it has to be. We can get an arrest warrant for you or you can just cooperate with us," Baynor said, grabbing onto Evelyn's arm.

"Wait! You don't understand!" Evelyn screamed. Detective Baynor wasn't letting up. She was pulling Evelyn towards her unmarked police car.

"Carolynn! Take the bag! Go get Arianna out! Please! Call the attorney! You can't do this to me! I didn't have anything to do with any of this!" Evelyn screeched. How did she go from victim of her husband's crimes to a suspect just like that? Detective Baynor and Ledbetter held onto Evelyn like she was a mass murderer as they escorted her to their waiting car.

"Mrs. Epstein…there are lots of stones unturned right now. We need to find out what happened to Shelby Frankel. We need to find out what you know about the murder of the main witness in your daughter's case. Your daughter is fighting for her freedom. And your husband is the most hated man in the United States right now. I guess this is what happens when you live rich and shameless," Detective Baynor said with a self-gratified tone lacing her words. The story of the rich and shameless Epsteins was far from over. In fact, it had really just begun.
Stay Tuned